TIDELINES

TIDELINES

Blair Carroll

Copyright © 2020 by Blair Carroll

All rights reserved. No part of this publication may be reproduced, distributed or transmitted in any form or by any means, without prior written permission.

This is a work of fiction. Names, characters, places, and incidents are a product of the author's imagination. Locales and public names are sometimes used for atmospheric purposes. Any resemblance to actual people, living or dead, or to businesses, companies, events, institutions, or locales is completely coincidental.

ISBN _____

This story is dedicated to BEKEM.
You know who you are.

CONTENTS

Prologue 11
PART ONE: ELSIE AND KATHERINE 13
   Chapter One: A Grim Discovery 15
   Chapter Two: Did He Catch a Fish? 19
   Chapter Three: The Beginning of a Beautiful Friendship 23
   Chapter Four: The Swimmer's Counsel 27
PART TWO: EMILY AND MADICAN 31
   Chapter Five: The Bracelet 33
   Chapter Six: The Pearl of New Orleans 37
   Chapter Seven: The Pirate Katherine 41
   Chapter Eight: I Can Read Your Thoughts, You Know 43
   Chapter Nine: It Was Safer That Way 46
   Chapter Ten: Lights and Eyelashes 53
   Chapter Eleven: A Grim Reminder 58
   Chapter Twelve: J L 61
   Chapter Thirteen: Stone Streets, Ghosts, and Gardens 64
   Chapter Fourteen: Jefferson and Michael 68
   Chapter Fifteen: There Was Nothing Anyone Could Do 72
   Chapter Sixteen: Daydreams 77
   Chapter Seventeen: Johnny Longskull Has a Heart 79
PART THREE: LAND RUNNERS VS SWIMMERS 83
   Chapter Eighteen: Oops 85
   Chapter Nineteen: Definitely Defensive Now 88
   Chapter Twenty: Don't Confuse Guilt with Grief and Worry ... 92
   Chapter Twenty-One: Spirits in the Sky 98
   Chapter Twenty-Two: Jean Lafitte 103

Chapter Twenty-Three: Demons and Ghosts 105

Chapter Twenty-Four: Salty Kisses 110

Chapter Twenty-Five: Meet Me Under the Crow's Nest 115

Chapter Twenty-Six: Help Is on the Horizon 120

Chapter Twenty-Seven: Fear the Swarm of Mermaids 123

Chapter Twenty-Eight: They're All on Their Way 125

Chapter Twenty-Nine: We'll Be There by Dusk 128

Chapter Thirty: Time to Get Dressed 130

Chapter Thirty-One: She's Not Going to Be Helping Us Today 135

Chapter Thirty-Two: A Big Family 139

Chapter Thirty-Three: MAN YOUR STATIONS! 144

Chapter Thirty-Four: Seaweed and Seashells 148

Chapter Thirty-Five: Bew's Curse 150

PART FOUR: IT'S THEIR SECRET TO SHARE 159

Chapter Thirty-Six: Smoke 161

Chapter Thirty-Seven: Don't Fear the Ocean 168

Epilogue 171

Prologue

Her swimming was smooth that morning. The water was calm and bright. Her movements were fluid and quick. She turned faster than any other Swimmer. She would bend her body like a dolphin and could obtain great speeds if she moved just slightly certain ways. She raced the dolphins and their tuna for fun. She could swim deeper than normal and still see. She loved days like this. She never tired of exploring the areas where they didn't normally go. It was not unlike her to venture off and get lost. She was credited for finding many species of fish no one knew existed before.

This morning, she swam further than normal, and saw the land coming into view. At the surface, she peeked her head out and saw a large ship in the distance. Her eyes took a minute to adjust to the light, but she could make it out clearly. It was one she had seen here before, and it was coming more frequently. She had seen it in battle with another ship, but most times she had seen it just sailing through the passage. These waters were hers and she felt very possessive, but she knew she couldn't take on a huge ship with Land Runners. Yet she was still very curious of them. It was her nature to be so questioning.

PART ONE:

ELSIE AND KATHERINE

Chapter One:
A Grim Discovery

Grim Blacktoad was an old ship's mate. He boasted having served on ten different vessels in his forty years of sailing with pirates. He had been a slave to the likes of the famous pirate Vincent Gambi and knew where Davey Jones' treasure was hidden. At least, he knew where it was before the other pirates found it. Otherwise, he would be a rich man with a vessel of his own.

Grim liked to share his tall tales over a pint. But most of his shipmates had heard his stories over and over so this night he was partaking of a pint on his own. The edge of the ship was lonely and quiet. So was the ocean. They'd sailed about three hundred miles off the coast in search of the King's fleet. If they could capture one of the ships in the fleet, they would all be rich, his pirate had promised. The truth was that Grim was lonely and quiet in his old age, just like the ship. He secretly longed to be on land, in a big house, in a warm bed, next to a good woman who loved him. Grim knew he'd never know that feeling. So, he kept drinking his pints and telling his stories. At least that gave him some pleasure, to see others laughing and smiling at the thought of finding Davey Jones' treasure. Grim peered out into the dark water. The moon was out that night, but there wasn't much to see.

Until he saw the flicker of glass in the water. It was like fluid glass. *Must be a jellyfish.* He had heard his own share of tall tales about mermaids in these waters, but he never thought they were true. But that glass, that liquid flowing glass, looked like hair on a woman's head. Grim had had several pints that night, so nothing was going to shock him. Just when he thought that to himself, he heard a woman's voice say, "I'm happy to share a pint with you." Grim turned around, thinking he heard the voice of his pirate captain, one of the only females on the ship, who was known to enjoy a pint with him every now and then. But no one was there.

Grim shook his head, thinking he must have imagined it. Until he heard her again. "You're not imagining anything. I'm down here in the water."

Grim was not shy and Grim was not afraid of much. But now, he was hesitant to look over the side into the dark water where the glass jellyfish creature was.

"Grim, if you help me aboard I'll be glad to share a pint with you."

This time Grim peered sheepishly over the side of the boat. There she was. Her head and shoulders were just out of the water. Her hair was clear like glass. It shimmered from the few candle lights that were on the boat. Her eyes were huge, and she was smiling. *She must be a mermaid.* Her smile was relaxing. He didn't feel scared at all after looking at her smile. She appeared happy to have someone talk to her. He knew that feeling well. As he held his hand out for her to climb up off the ladder he said, "If you come aboard, you'll have to be quiet." *Really?* He thought to himself. *That's what you say to a mermaid?* He knew he should be asking her all kinds of questions. He knew he should be in awe of this amazing creature. But he just couldn't bring himself to do anything but stare at her smile and talk as if this was no big deal at all.

No, she didn't have a fish tail. She had legs. *Of course she does*, he thought to himself. She wore a green wrap around her body. Almost like seaweed. It was dark green and looked slimy.

"This helps me swim through the water easier," she answered his thought.

"Um…" he began.

"Don't worry, I know you have many questions for me. And I have many for you too."

All Grim could do was hold out his hand and offer her a pint. She graciously accepted the mug while he motioned to a couple of small stools and they sat down, both eager to learn about each other. They talked into the night. He learned so much about her. There was a whole area nearby of mermaids, or Swimmers, as they preferred to be called. Her family lived nearby. Her name was Elsie. She was married to Samuel. Elsie told him the Swimmers could communicate through a type of telepathy. There was no problem under water, but above water it was tricky because their thoughts had to "bounce" off something in order for it to work. So, she could hear his thoughts when she concentrated enough. But he could only hear hers if she let him. She also explained that she had more webbing between her fingers and toes than Land Runners because it helped her swim.

They laughed at the idea of the drawings they'd seen of how Land Runners envisioned mermaids. Fish tails! How funny that sounded! Swimmers looked very much like Land Runners. They came from the same beginnings. He learned Elsie was one of a few Swimmers who wanted their civilizations to know about each other and to learn from each other. Most Swimmers wanted to keep their presence a secret for safety sake because they were ultimately scared of the Land Runners. But the Swimmers could stay on land for long periods of time, and often came ashore to mingle with the Land Runners and learn more about them. They'd developed the ability to survive above or below the surface. She was sad that the Land Runners could only live above the surface.

She told him of the Ama divers in Japan, a land he had not been to yet but decided he needed to go. Those divers would train to hold their breath for long periods of time so they could stay under water searching for pearls. She told him that Swimmers often helped new Ama divers find the pearls.

It was a rough life for those women and they were often enslaved into finding treasures for their men. The Swimmers felt bad for them and often helped them. The Ama divers did not know them as Swimmers. They thought they were the ghosts of their ancestors coming to help them. Grim thought about his ancestors who died in prisons and wondered if their ghosts were around trying to help him with this treasure. The more he listened to her talk the more he realized the true treasure he had found. He imagined bringing her before the King of Spain and offering her as a gift. Surely, he'd be rewarded for that! Elsie wasn't paying attention when he thought about the beautiful mermaid wrapped up in a cage being presented to the King. She was not being careful. She was too excited and this seemed to be going so well.

Dawn was breaking and he was concerned someone would find her. This was one treasure he would keep to himself. He wanted to make sure his pirate captain knew about her, that he had found, er, ah, captured her and that she could make them rich.

A GRIM DISCOVERY

"Elsie, the other men and women will be awaking soon. I think it may be for the best to hide you for a while. Just until I can tell my captain about you. She may not be as gracious or calm about you as I was." He grinned a rather large prideful grin. Elsie smiled at his sense of self-worth and agreed to go below deck with him to hide for now. Off the back deck was a storage compartment. This is where Grim made sure the loading boys put the extra rum before setting sail. There were also old wooden crates that had been emptied out during the journey so far.

These crates would be filled back up when they reached the next port. So, it was wise to keep them. As they made their way down into the hole, Grim motioned to the back corner of the room for Elsie to go hide for now. She was very excited about the possibility of meeting the captain of the ship and knew this would be the start of a great relationship between the two worlds. That is until she felt the sharp pain on the back of her head. Grim had knocked her out cold.

Grim knew it wouldn't be long before she woke up and started howling. What a find! He would be so rich! His pirate captain would be so proud! He made sure she was breathing, and then he tied her arms and legs, gagged her mouth and put her into the medium-size crate. He tied rope around it so she could not get out if she woke up. Then he went upstairs on deck to find his captain and let her know about his "catch."

Chapter Two:
Did He Catch a Fish?

Katharine was tall for a woman. And striking. And when men called her striking what they meant was intimidating. She was so beautiful that it scared most men away. She was so exotic looking that it scared most women away. That morning, the sun was bright. She knew they had a lot of sailing to do that day if they wanted to keep up with their route. Since her old captain, Kay Lee, had died Katharine had become the captain of *The Black Susan*, the fastest pirate ship in the Caribbean. She had a crew of fifty men and women who were very loyal to her and believed in her vision. They'd been with her on the last three takeovers and she was fair to all of them. She believed in hard work, but she also believed in treating her team to a large portion of the collection.

She had adopted Kay Lee's love of the thievery for the sake of the beauty in the item. She robbed others because she liked what she obtained. She didn't do it because she made money, because she had plenty of money. She just took what she liked and gave the rest to the crew.

That kept them very happy, and very loyal.

The men were already working on turning the ship toward home. This had been a short trip and she was eager to get home to deliver the supplies. She knew once she dropped off the supplies her island family needed, she would have time to travel to Barataria to see Jean Lafitte. She had just started daydreaming about him when Grim approached her from behind.

"Captain, I wonder if I might have a moment to show you a treasure I found for you last night." Grim was twisting his hat in his hands.

"Grim, I hope you are not going to show me your hat because it looks as if you've killed it." Katharine smirked at him.

"Oh, no, ma'am," Grim corrected. "The treasure is actually down in the galley."

"Fine, lead the way," Katharine agreed. Grim led her to the end of the boat and down to stairwell into the hull. The hull was dark and wet and Katharine's eyes had not adjusted enough when she heard a muffled rattling at the other end.

"Grim, what are you bringing me to see?" she asked, a bit concerned.

"Ma'am, I know you won't believe it if I told you what I found, I mean caught, last night. So, I just need to show you." He took her by the elbow and tried to lead her. Katharine was too smart not to be cautious. She pulled away from his grasp but ventured forward, as if to let him lead her toward the back.

More muffled came an "Mmmmm, mmmmm." The noise sounded louder now. There was thumping and something was obviously thrashing around. *Did he catch a fish?* She thought to herself.

"Please help me," a voice spoke to her mind. Katharine shook it off, thinking she was possessed.

"What's going on?" she said to Grim, a bit too scared to go any further.

"Please, ma'am. Just a little closer."

Katharine started to make out what she never expected. There, in the middle of the barrels and crates, was one medium-size crate. And the strange muffled noise was coming from inside that crate. Katharine quickened her steps, fearing the worse, and stopped at the crate. She summoned her inner strength and tore off the ropes. Carefully and slowly she opened the lid.

Inside she saw a nightmare—a woman bound and gagged.

"Grim! What have you done?" She growled and yelled at him at the same time. She immediately reached for the woman to begin to take her gag out of her mouth. As soon as she touched the woman a whirlwind of images and sounds flooded her mind. There were visions of undersea life, a man swimming with dolphins, a young boy swimming with the woman. Light from above floating down through the water. *Painful headache, can't breathe. I need the water.* Katharine fell to her knees as the woman screamed. It was more of a shrill call like from a whale. The woman attempted to stand in the crate and Katharine moved to help her.

Grim was not sure what to do. He started to back away. "Don't move," Katharine growled. Grim froze in his tracks while Katharine leaned into the woman and helped her out of the crate. She untied her and sat her down. The woman was scared and shaking. Katharine could tell she was sick. "Please, I need water," she heard in her mind. Several shipmates had made their way into the supply room and had stopped in their tracks, not sure what to make of this woman with the glass-like hair.

Katharine yelled, "Go fetch this woman some water!" No one moved. "Now!" she barked.

One of the shipmates ran off. Katharine kneeled in front of the woman and peered into her eyes. The woman tried to look away but, when their eyes finally met, they both felt at ease.

Katharine knew this poor woman had been captured by Grim and needed water fast. The woman knew Katharine was going to help her, not hurt her. She had let her guard down before, but never again. Slowly Katharine leaned into the woman and held her. The woman returned the connection. After a minute, Katharine let go and stood up. Slowly she turned toward Grim.

The young shipmate was just returning with a pint of what Katharine seriously hoped was water. She looked at the shipmate and motioned toward the woman. Fearfully he made his way to the odd-looking woman and handed her the water. She took the mug without hesitation and gulped down most of it. The rest she poured over her head.

Katharine's intense stare went immediately back to Grim. He was standing up with slumped shoulders and his head was hanging low. He was trying to slowly back away.

"You are an idiot," she articulated to Grim. "How dare you capture this poor woman for your self-interest and wealth? I refuse to promote such cruelty. You are relieved of your duty on my ship."

Grim looked up, shocked at her words. "B-b-b-b-but, we're not docked, ma'am." He feared she would throw him overboard.

"Jim, Steve, take this man up to my cabin." Katharine stood stoic as the two shipmates grabbed Grim by his arms and led him out of the storage area. She could hear others hovering, whispering. She knew she couldn't keep this secret, but knew she had to let this woman go. She didn't want to seem weak in front of her crew. She turned back toward the woman and sat down next to her.

"Can you speak?" Katharine decided to go slowly with the questions.

"Yes," the woman answered. "But you can hear me in your head, can't you?"

DID HE CATCH A FISH?

Katharine avoided that question and instead asked, "What is your name?"

"Elsie."

"How did you get here?" was Katharine's next question. Elsie proceeded to tell Katharine everything about her attempt to meet a Land Runner. She started talking and talking and before she knew it she had told Katharine everything about the Swimmers. Katharine was not shocked. She had heard rumors about mermaids before and she often had feelings that they watched her ships. The two women sat for an hour learning about each other. Katharine was as fascinated with Elsie as Elsie was with her. Elsie felt more at ease with Katharine and because she could read her thoughts she knew Katharine was not going to hurt or betray her.

She also knew Katharine could keep a secret.

The two were interrupted by the shipmate Steve. "Captain, we are still heading toward the Isle of Bryce. Do you wish to continue in this direction?"

Katharine rubbed her eyes and realized that the ship had been traveling all night. They were probably a great distance from Elsie's home and she wasn't sure if they should turn back.

"It's all right, Katharine. My husband Samuel has been with us the whole time," Elsie spoke to Katharine's thoughts. Katharine was beginning to accept this ability.

"Okay," she thought to herself. Katharine wondered why her husband didn't try to board the ship to save his wife.

"He can't take on a ship this size." Elsie explained in Katharine's mind. She continued, "It was forbidden for me to contact Land Runners, but I did it anyway. Samuel was trying to find a way to rescue me without the others finding out."

Katharine thought she understood that explanation but then asked, "Should we slow our pace a bit?"

"Yes, that would be appreciated," Elsie answered.

"Yes, thank you," a male voice spoke in Katharine's head. Katharine was startled but laughed out loud.

"Was that Samuel?" she asked.

"Yes, it's me," the voice answered. Katharine continued to laugh.

"I'm not Samuel," said the shipmate, obviously confused now and still waiting for Katharine to answer.

TIDELINES

Chapter Three:
The Beginning of a Beautiful Friendship

The Black Susan had lowered most of her sails and charted a slower course back to the Isle of Bryce. Katharine frequented the waters in the Caribbean during her visits to Jean Lafitte, and while scouting for ships to rob. When she wasn't pirating she lived on her small island located off the coast of South Florida near Haiti. Many pirates used that waterway as they traveled to the middle Americas. That evening, she had company in her dining chambers. Elsie and Samuel were aboard the ship offering some explanation about their lives. Katharine was entranced by the two Swimmers and eagerly listened to them explain about themselves.

"When the world was born and man began to walk, he saw there were vast lands for him to explore. The birds and the trees called to him. He felt at home among the rocky, dirty soil. His feet grew strong and stiff. His legs were steady and he could run." Elsie smiled and stood up. She walked to the edge of the cabin and looked out the window hole. "The world he could see was his to own and manage. However, not all men were steady on their legs. They turned away from the dirty soil and chose a home in the cool waters, tempted to explore what must be called the unknown, the area under the rippling reflective surface, the area past the tide lines. Some men, our ancestors, chose to make their home there." She turned and sat back down.

Samuel continued. "The world became a small place very soon. Some men made great cities under water. We call ourselves Swimmers and live mostly in the water, but obviously we can spend some time out of the water too. We learned how to live in peace and away from the men who lived only on the land whom we call the Land Runners." Samuel stopped and looked at Katharine who was sitting on her bench leaning in with her head in her hands. It occurred to her that she had stumbled upon something amazing so she was concentrating on every word.

"Most land masses were quickly inhabited by Land Runners. They made cities, and large communities, they fought over things and killed each other. Sometimes they ventured out into the oceans to move from one land to another. This didn't bother the Swimmers in the early years because their contact was very rare. The Swimmers wanted to keep their survival to themselves. The Land Runners were much stronger. The Swimmers felt that the Land Runners would try to conquer their homes underwater, as they had done to each other on land. So, for the sake of survival, the Swimmers kept to themselves and didn't let the Land Runners know they existed. Then Land Runners began to develop ideas about gods and mythic creatures. They developed stories about creatures they swore existed. Including the Swimmers whom they call mermaids."

Katharine listened intently, taking it all in. She was overwhelmed at knowing she was learning something that no other human, or Land Runner, had learned before. She shook her head and a small chuckle came over her. Elsie read her thoughts and knew Katharine was trustworthy and willing to share her life with them. She knew the two would be bonded forever.

"Some Swimmers had been careless over the thousands of years and had let themselves be seen. The rumor that these fish-human creatures living under water began to expand, especially in fishing towns. However, it was still just that, a rumor. While living in the water we developed other things besides strong stiff feet like our brothers on land. Over thousands of years, our species grew small webbing between our fingers and toes that helped us maneuver under water." Elsie showed her hand and Samuel's hand to Katharine who stared at the little bit of clear skin between each finger. Then Elsie spoke to Katharine's thoughts. "We also developed the ability to communicate through a type of telepathy. We use sound bumps to send messages to others. It works like sending tiny little pulses under water. Each pulse is unique and represents a different word. We've also developed this ability above water."

Samuel continued, "Our skin became less porous and more pliable. This lets us store fat, like the whale's blubber when traveling to colder waters. We have two different ways to breath that enable us to live above and below the surface. But we choose to stay under as much as possible."

Katharine was overwhelmed, which didn't happen to her very often. All she could think of to say was, "I'm anxious for you to see my home. I have so much to share with you too."

"We're looking forward to meeting everyone." Elsie responded.

"It's a beautiful island, thick with greenery on the inside and rocky along the outside. Deep inside there is a stream formed from a fresh water spring. The stream makes its way down through the trees and opens into a small pool before cascading into a brief waterfall." Katharine used her hands to make the flowing motion like a river. "The small river pushes through the undergrowth and is eventually filtered underground by the large rocks that form the cliffs. On one side of the island is a clearing. This is where I've made my home and where the town is located. Our island is very modern. I've collected some beautiful things that I share with everyone." Katharine stopped for a moment and closed her eyes. She thought about her beautiful island home and how much she missed it when she was not there.

"It sounds lovely, Katharine. And Samuel and I are thrilled that you are allowing us to visit." She smiled at Katharine.

"Elsie, I want you to know that the islanders are very loyal to me. And so are the crew members of this ship. I keep them well fed and clothed, and I provide beautiful and often rare items for them to trade." She stopped, trying to find the right words, then continued, "These people are my family. They value the relationships we have developed. Most were running from something. Some were falsely accused of a crime, or just simply trying to find a better way of life. They will welcome you without judgement and without expectations of violating your secret."

"Thank you." Elsie smiled. "We are anxious for the Land Runners to understand us and know us. But the counsel doesn't agree. They are too concerned that Land Runners are too violent and would take advantage of us." Elsie stopped and glanced at Samuel, whose mouth was puckering in disapproval. He knew the stubbornness of his wife, and knew this violation of the counsel was not going to be a good move. But he loved her too much, and deep inside he agreed with her desire to know the Land Runners better.

Elsie continued, breaking off the stare from her husband, "But maybe this is a good way for us to start. Maybe our relationship, our new friendship, can prove to them Land Runners and Swimmers can live peacefully." Elsie reached for Katharine's hand and gave it a squeeze.

THE BEGINNING OF A BEAUTIFUL FRIENDSHIP

Katharine gave a slight smile to Samuel, hoping he'd be as convinced as she and Elsie were that the two groups should mingle.

Chapter Four:
The Swimmer's Counsel

Katharine's ship had continued sailing toward the Isle of Bryce. It would take several days to make it home. Samuel and Elsie stayed close, but traveled in the water. They came aboard every evening to talk with Katharine and other crew members about their life under the surface. The crew would gather on the main deck sitting wherever there was room with their backs against the railing of the ship. They were fascinated and asked the two many questions. They wanted to know about the cities and where they were, and how many Swimmers were there, and how they were able to read minds. But mostly they just wanted to know "why now?"

Steve spoke up. "Why are you now ready to make yourselves known? You've lived in peace and quiet and anonymity for so long."

Elsie spoke first "Well, honestly, Samuel was not really okay with my wanting to meet you." Some of the crew shifted in their seats, curious as to what that really meant. Elsie noticed their uneasiness and corrected herself. "He wanted to meet everyone and have our worlds know each other. He just wanted a better way to go about it. I was the one who was insistent upon doing it our way."

"Yes, and it almost got you killed." Samuel slightly scolded his better half, knowing he could in no way control her any more than the beaches control the tides.

"We talked to the counsel first, but they didn't see things the way we did." Elsie explained.

She remembered the night of the council meeting.

"Our worlds are getting too close. It's time we let them know we're here." Samuel had been first to say what they were all thinking. He was always the one in the crowd to speak up, to lead the group. He had been on the counsel for only a year and was not considered full rank yet, but nonetheless he spoke.

Others gasped, and countered, "They could kill us as easily as we kill the plankton and the sardine!"

"We wouldn't stand a chance," argued McCade, the oldest on the counsel.

"I don't believe that," Samuel insisted. "I've been among them. There are many good people. If we do this the right way we could ensure our world would be free of any danger they could impose."

"And just how do you propose we do that? We can't just swim up to them and say, 'Oh, hello, I'm what you call a mermaid, and there are thousands of us living under water just like there are thousands of you living on land. We want to be your friend,'" Blake said with a smirk. She was very pessimistic.

"Actually," Samuel continued, "I was thinking about letting one of the vessels catch us. You know, make it look like it was their doing. Then we would show them we meant no harm. Oh, they would be scared at first, but soon they would see we're creatures in this world just like them. Heck, we came from the same ancestors!"

"I just don't think it's a good idea," Carter pleaded. He was on the planning committee in charge of building new homes and cities. "If something happened to you, or any of us, it could mean the end of all of us. I think we should spend more time studying these vessels first and maybe we can determine why they are here and what they are doing before announcing ourselves."

The Swimmers had debated this issue into the evening and finally put it to rest, agreeing that more studying should go on before entering into any kind of announcement of their species. Many had seen battles take place amongst the Land Runners and feared that kind of horror could befall them as well.

Samuel made his way home and discussed the evening's talks with Elsie. She was much more outspoken than Samuel, and braver when it came to actually following through. She insisted it was time to talk to the Land Runners. She was excited about the adventure and the new way of life that might be for them. She felt it was time to merge the civilizations. And she thought she was just the Swimmer to do it!

"Sam, I knew you wouldn't get anywhere with those old Swimmers. They are too old fashioned to make any changes."

TIDELINES

"I know but…"

"But nothing! You are never going to change their mind. We're going to have to take on this kind of thing ourselves."

"Elsie, I know you feel strongly about this. But think about what you're saying. We can't just take it upon ourselves to start a line of communication with the Land Runners. That's crazy!"

"Is it? Is it crazy, Sam? Who else is going to do it? When the counsel does decide eventually that we need to introduce ourselves, someone is going to have to do it."

"I know. But why does it have to be you or me? Think about Madican."

Madican was their son, who was three years old. He was very adventurous like his mother and extremely strong and smart like his father. The combination was hazardous.

"What about Madican? I actually think it would be good for him to learn another culture. Imagine the knowledge he could gain from running with a bunch of Land Runner boys."

"You are so hard headed, Elsie." Sam smiled and held her in his arms.

"Sam, what if we met a Land Runner and started talking to them?"

"We've met them and we've talked to them. They just didn't know it was a Swimmer they were talking too."

"Yeah, so what if we started talking to them, built up some camaraderie with them and then let them know who we were." She smiled her sweet smile into his eyes, hoping she could convince him.

"No."

THE SWIMMER'S COUNSEL

PART TWO:

EMILY AND MADICAN

Chapter Five:
The Bracelet

It was a sun-bleached morning on the Isle of Bryce. Emily and Madican were running along the ocean. "Okay, Mad, try to keep up!" Emily ran for the love of it. She had done it for as long as she could remember. Maybe that was why she ran—to remember. Or maybe it was to forget. Either way it cleared her mind and kept her sharp. Madican ran because she told him too. He would do anything for Emily.

When he was almost four, his mom, Elsie, had brought him to the island and introduced them. Right away he knew Emily was a special person and they were instant best friends. Now that she had grown into a young woman, he began to notice how beautiful she looked. Her hair was the color of a coconut's shell, and her eyes were as bright as the blue tang fish. He liked to think she was the best of both the Swimmer's world and the Land Runner's world. He loved the way she read his thoughts so easily for a Land Runner. He didn't have to concentrate that hard, it was like they had a special connection. Emily loved Madican like a brother. He was the only person close to her age on that island. She felt he was special too. She had prayed for a friend, like a sister. But when she met Madican, she figured God didn't hear the sister part.

Running helped him strengthen his walk, and that was important if he was to continue to hide amongst the Land Runners and pretend to be one of them. Swimmers never lost their ability to walk on land. They just weren't all that good at it. Some were better than others so they were chosen to pretend to be Land Runners and go ashore to investigate them.

Madican's mother, Elsie, had become friends with Katharine 12 years ago, when he had first come to the island. Katharine told Elsie that she and her family could walk amongst Katharine's townspeople on the island anytime they chose. The residents of Katharine's island town were loyal and knew it was best to keep the secret.

"Emily, you know I can't run as fast as you!" Madican yelled back at her. Emily knew he couldn't, but she liked teasing him. She grinned to herself then slowed her pace slightly so he could catch up. He matched her gait then pushed ahead of her, smiling back at her as he ran. "Oh, he really is nice to look at" she thought as his shoulder-length hair bounced in time with each step. Deep down she knew she would do anything for him too. Swimmers' hair is not like Land Runners. It's more like the scales of a fish, translucent and opulent, but flexible enough so it almost moves like real hair. To a passerby it may seem odd. But if Swimmers are on land they keep it hidden, or dyed, so they won't draw attention. Here, on their beach, Madican did not have to hide anything from Emily. She knew all about his hair. And his thoughts. They loved this part of the beach where the ocean leaned in and kissed it.

The sand on the tide line there was smooth and clean and packed. It was perfect for running. Madican told her about the different places in the world he had visited, and he would bring her treasures from each place. Her favorite was the bracelet he found at the wreckage of the *Atocha*, part of a fleet of twenty-one ships that had sunken off the coast of Florida about two hundred years ago. He told her that the skeletons of the soldiers who manned the ship were still in the hull at the bottom of the ocean. She didn't believe that tale, but she loved to wear the bracelet. The silver band was thin and solid. The clasp was unusual with two hands that slid together to hold the bracelet on her wrist. The shiny object was a compliment against her tan skin and it looked like it was made just for her. Another islander, Pearl, who was like a grandmother to her, said it was too fancy and didn't match anything so wore, but Emily didn't care. She just loved it that Madican thought of her enough to bring her beautiful things and share his world with her.

When Swimmers wanted to they could travel far distances very fast. They would hit the right current jet stream and it would take them thousands of miles in a short amount of time. Madican's mother, Elsie, had been an investigator for the Swimmers. Her job was to travel to different areas and secretly learn about the Land Runners. Emily's favorite story was when Elsie helped save the life of an enslaved Ama Diver from Japan. To Emily Japan seemed so far away, but to a Swimmer, it seemed like it was right next door. Elsie had made a crucial mistake and let her

TIDELINES

presence be known when one of the divers saw her. The diver panicked, thinking it was the spirit of her ancestor coming back to punish her. The woman began to go into shock under water! Elsie knew the woman couldn't breathe so she allowed her to read her thoughts. This was a dangerous and forbidden thing to do for a Swimmer. But Elsie couldn't let the woman drown! She told the woman to stay calm and Elsie raced her to the top of the water. She held the woman out of the water until the woman began to breathe on her own. Then she floated her to the edge of the ocean where the water meets the sand and watched until her captor found her.

Elsie watched as the man checked the woman's bag for shells first, then he checked to see if she was still breathing. When he found she was still alive, he became angry with her. To him, she had tarnished his honor by not finding any shells for him. In his opinion if she couldn't do her job, she should have died. But he too thought the ancestors had intervened so, not wanting to disappoint them, he left her there instead of killing her. Elsie watched, confused, while he walked away from her. Eventually the woman woke up and stumbled away on her own. This story always made Emily wonder about the true nature of people.

Emily slowed her pace and came to a stop. Leaning over she put her hands on her knees and breathed hard. "That was fun," she thought. Madican heard her and stopped too. He walked back to her and they both plopped down in the sand. "Is Katharine coming back today?" He asked. "Yeah, she is supposed to be back on the thirtieth day. I miss her when she isn't around."

"Why don't you ever go with her?" Madican asked.

"You know why, Mad," Emily looked down at her toes pushing mounds in the sand.

"You're going to have to face this sometime, Em. You can't stay on this island forever. Remember, I can read your thoughts and I know you want to see all those places I tell you about."

She hated it when he was right. "I know. I'm just not ready yet."

"You'll have to get over this fear, Emily," Madican insisted. Emily hung her head and turned away. "I know." She whispered to herself. Her memory was still too vivid to forget everything that happened.

The trip was supposed to take them to another place to live, her parents had explained. They were going to start fresh. She had understood very little at that age. At

THE BRACELET

only two and a half years old she really didn't understand why they were leaving, just that she would follow her family anywhere. The ship was much larger than she had imagined. Her family lived further inland and she had never seen the ocean or a big ship before. The smell of the salt and rotting fish didn't really bother her. It had been something new to experience.

But when she saw the ocean, its darkness was intimidating. She was scared to go toward it. Her parents assured her it was okay, they even told her the ship was like a big castle, full of rooms to explore. She held her father's hand tight as she walked the long board to the ship. The wood was dirty and it smelled bad. There was a lot of large crates and ropes everywhere. And the men didn't have any shirts on. They ran from one end of the ship to the other, picking up ropes and yelling at each other. It was not like a castle at all. Her family was led inside the ship to a dark wet room. They lit a small lantern and looked around. There were two benches and slick sticky wetness on the floor and walls. She started to cry. Her parents held her tight and she cried herself to sleep.

When she began to wake, she remembered a feeling of warmth in her mother's arms, but it was quickly overshadowed by the stench of the small room. She opened her eyes and couldn't see much, the lantern was not lit. "Shhh," her mother calmed her. "Did you sleep okay?" Emily just looked around to make sure her dad was there. She found him slumped on the bench across from them. "Daddy?" she asked. "He's trying to sleep," her mother answered. She nestled into her mother and thought about the new place they were going to. Maybe her mother meant they were going to a castle, because this ship certainly was nothing like a castle.

"It's okay, you know I would go with you. I would be with you the whole time." Madican put his hand on top of hers. Careful not to hold it, just touch it, so she'd know he was there. She didn't flinch this time and actually smiled. "I know," she responded, "I promise you'll be the first to know when I'm ready."

That was good for now. He didn't want to push the issue. So, he decided to change the subject. "I'm starving. Does Pearl have any tenderloin today?" He asked.

"Mad, if you want tenderloin you know she'll make it for you."

"Good, let's go check." He was quick to get up so he could help her up. But she didn't let him. She rose on her own and started walking toward the town, heading for the tavern where Pearl worked.

Chapter Six:
The Pearl of New Orleans

Pearl had been raised on a large sugar cane plantation outside of New Orleans, Louisiana. Although she was raised as a member of the family, she had actually been born into slavery. Her mother was a slave, but her daddy was a young man of the house. When her mother died in childbirth, her father brought her into the big house to live. Most members of the family were not kind to her so she spent most of her day with the slaves and picked up many of their practices. One day, the magistrate accused her—along with many other women from the area—of practicing voodoo. This was a common practice amongst the slaves and the people who lived in the swamps, but not for the wealthy. However, signs of the practice had been showing up lately in the shops on St. Charles Street and the local townspeople were fearful of it. People had seen Pearl making potions from strange herbs and thought she would use them to turn everyone into different kinds of animals.

Pearl had a large garden that she used to grow many different things. Pearl never confessed nor denied practicing voodoo. When it became clear she would likely do time for her "crime", she decided to run. It was not like her to run away from anything. But there was no hope for her amongst the people of New Orleans. They had already made up their minds and they needed someone to blame for the encroaching practices. They knew very little about voodoo and, rather than study it, they shunned it and feared it and made it into something to be afraid of, something bad.

She knew she could not escape the magistrate's opinion once it was already made up. Her only escape was to stowaway on a ship bound for England. But that ship didn't make it. It was lost at sea in a storm. Pearl was the only survivor. Holding tight to a board, she was found floating in the ocean by Katharine. Pearl invented a name and a made-up family who she claimed all perished in the sunken ship. Katharine offered to take her with them as a member of her crew and Pearl agreed, knowing she really didn't have another option. While on their journey, the crew began to suffer from an unknown ailment that caused severe abdominal cramping and fever. Pearl was able to use her knowledge of plants and potions to make a brew that cured the crew members. From then on Katharine respected Pearl as a healer and someone to be trusted.

Katharine knew Pearl had a secret surrounding her knowledge of these potions and herbs. But she was intrigued rather than fearful. She thought whatever Pearl was doing must be good because she had saved her crew. However, Pearl didn't like the life of a pirate and asked to stay ashore. Katharine agreed to let her stay at her island and keep watch on things while she was gone.

Pearl took this new responsibility and life style seriously. She adapted well to the island and the small group of residents who lived there. Because she was able to heal people, they looked to her as a type of doctor or medicine woman. Her respect grew and eventually she became the leader of the island when Katharine was away. Her love for cooking led her to work at Jesse's Place, the local tavern of sorts that all the islanders frequented. The tavern didn't have a name, people just called it Jesse's place, after Jesse, who ran it. It soon became the stopping point for many pirates coming in and out of the passage. After Jesse died, Pearl took over, but kept the name the same.

Pearl doted on all the children of the island, but she was especially fond of their frequent guests, Madican and his sister, Bew. Bew loved pork ribs and Madican loved tenderloin. When they came to visit the island, she would always make sure to prepare a hog just for them. Living in the water, it was hard to come by a good pork roast.

Pearl was busy pouring rum for Johnny Longskull and two of his men when Emily and Madican walked up to the tavern fresh from their run. The rum Katharine made on her island was the most coveted in the world. She brought in fresh cane from Louisiana and molasses from Brazil. Longskull bought the most, as his crew loved to drink. They didn't do much pirating anymore. They just stole enough to buy more rum. It was a constant cycle, but Longskull was a friend so Katharine obliged.

Bew was at the end of the bar chomping on ribs. When she saw Emily, she giggled and hollered "Em-uh-lee!!!! Come here, come here, come here!" Emily made her way through the people and put her arm around Bew. "These are amazing! Pearl is the very best cook!" Bew shot a glance toward Pearl who just smiled as she handed another group of men a plate of biscuits.

"Here's to Pearl!" One scalawag raised his glass in response to Bew.

"Here! Here!" was the raucous reply. In these waters, there were three women you best respect if you were on a pirate ship—Katharine, Pearl, and Bew. Katharine kept the waters safe for the pirates to pass through by maintaining the lighthouse and the trading post on her island. And she brought in her fair share of treasure for bargaining and trading. Pearl was the best cook on any island. If you wanted to keep a pirate happy, keep him fed, well-fed. And Bew? Well, Bew was the little girl who reminded all the pirates of their own little girls. Those they had met, those they hadn't, and those they had lost. Every pirate loved Bew.

Jesse's Place was not the same as other dives these pirates would frequent. It was solace from the wild behavior the pirates found other places. Here they got good food and sweet songs. They were reminded of families and the lives they had left on the mainland to take on this life of thievery. Those were protected, secret memories they all had, but wouldn't admit to. It was a respected place they guarded well. It was, in a sense, their church.

Emily and Madican sat down next to Bew. "What's on the menu today, Pearl?" Madican asked.

"Well, child, what are you thinking you might like old Pearl to whip up for you?" Pearl winked at him. She was beginning to think a lot about the fact that Emily was getting older. Emily had come to Pearl when she was not quite three. She would be wanting a boyfriend soon. Pearl watched her friendship with Madican and feared it might develop into something more. But Elsie assured her it would never happen. A Land Runner and a Swimmer should not be married. It wouldn't work out. Their worlds were too different. But Pearl wasn't so sure. She saw the way Madican looked at Emily. He really loved her, even if he didn't know it yet. But for now, she was glad Emily had a friend. Even if he was what people called a mermaid.

Madican tilted his head, made his eyes sparkle, and asked, "Do you have any tenderloin?"

Pearl just huffed as if he had insulted her, then laughed and said, "For you? Let me just go check my stockroom." And she wiggled off back to the back room of the tavern, laughing out loud the whole way. Emily reached over and helped herself to one of Bew's pork ribs. Bew just giggled more when Emily tried to put the whole thing in her mouth.

"Pearl, any news from Katharine?" Emily hollered toward Pearl in the back.

"Yeah, or from my mom?" Madican added.

"No, not yet. I suppose she is going to be rolling in here maybe tomorrow." Pearl yelled her answer from the back.

The islanders were used to Katharine being gone for periods of time. But lately Emily was really missing her when she was gone. Emily had feelings and ideas she wanted a woman's opinion on. Katharine wasn't much of a talker, and usually Emily did all the talking and Katharine just listened, allowing Emily a chance to work out whatever issues she was having herself. Today she was thinking about her feelings toward Madican. Why he touched her hand and why he looked at her the way he did sometimes. She really couldn't wait until Katharine got home.

Chapter Seven:
The Pirate Katherine

Katharine had been raised in South America by a small tribe. She had been born a long baby, so long that the tribal council called her cursed and wanted to sacrifice her to the gods. But her mother pleaded for her life. She promised her daughter would bring good fortune to the tribe. And since her mother was in good favor with one of the high priests, they agreed to let her live. The only stipulation was that she be raised like a boy.

So, Katharine was called "Tacito" by the tribe and trained to be a warrior, all the time having to hide the fact that she was a girl. Unfortunately, when young girls grow up they can't hide certain physical features that develop. When the other boys found out she was really a girl, their anger and fear overcame them and they beat her. She was cast out of the tribe at twelve years old. She ran away into the jungle, but easily survived using the skills she had learned all her life. She made her way to Brazil and finally into Central America where she began living as a thief in Coast Rica. Katharine used the skills she had acquired by living as a "boy" to find work on ships sailing to the Americas. She made her living as a ship's mate for a while until she was found out by Kay Lee, a long-time pirate who robbed cargo ships in the Caribbean.

Kay Lee's crew had overtaken one of the ships Katharine was on. Katharine used to fight alongside her fellow sailors, all the time dressed like a man. Kay Lee had come across the merchant vessel Katharine had been working on for three months. Kay Lee had been told the ship was secretly carrying four large solid silver candelabras, which she desperately desired because she thought they would look nice when she dined.

Kay Lee did not believe in killing anyone she didn't have to. So, instead they would make the shipmates on the captured ship strip to their undergarments and toss them overboard to survive, maybe, the waters of whatever ocean she happened to be on. That day, Katharine was on the losing ship. When asked to strip down to her underwear, Katharine protested. Kay Lee stared at her for a minute then began to laugh, immediately recognizing what all the other shipmates didn't—that Katharine was a woman. Kay Lee could hardly control herself and eventually Katharine began to laugh too, not sure what else to do. Kay Lee ordered Katharine to be taken to her quarters and she would deal with "him" after she made the others jump overboard.

Later in Kay Lee's quarters, Katharine told her the story of her life in the tribe and how she was surviving now. Kay Lee was much older than Katharine and took a liking to her, as if she were a little sister. Kay Lee began teaching Katharine the way of the pirate.

Katharine liked how easy it was to just climb aboard and take over a ship. Most men didn't know what to think of a female pirate so they tended to give up pretty easily. But besides not liking to kill anyone either, Katharine didn't like to take everything they had, and would often leave half the treasure behind in hopes that some of those who were sent overboard might survive to make use of it. She convinced Kay Lee it was so the crew could invest the money, make more money, and live to be robbed another day. Kay Lee would laugh at Katharine's attempt to hide her sensitivity and go along with it, just happy to have a companion.

One summer Kay Lee took Katharine back to her tribe. The elders were gone, and her mother had long since passed away, but the boys she had grown up with were still there. At least they were until Kay Lee arrived.

Chapter Eight:
I Can Read Your Thoughts, You Know

Katharine had been back for two days when Emily finally found time to see the items in the village. Katharine brought new things every time she came back, but Emily was usually too busy helping Pearl with Jesse's Place that she had little time to see all the items. Normally when Katharine arrived, many islanders would help unload the supplies and filter everything where it needed to go—chickens to the coop, hogs to the hidden caves, cane and molasses into the thick jungle inside the island where the rum was made. Everyone had a job to do. The residents of the island would all do their part to support their community. They grew tropical crops, mostly fruit, and raised hogs and chickens, and, most importantly, they made rum.

The town had a central area with a well. The shops circled this area and the homes split off from the center. There were sandy paths and green foliage sprouted up in some areas between the few shops and the small huts. The contrasting image of tan sand and green grasses was beautiful. A few flowering bougainvillea would spot the greenery and make it breathtaking. Emily loved her home. The lighthouse sat about one hundred yards up the hill from the center of the town, and Jesse's Place was on the other side of the town on an opposite hill. Their homes were cleverly designed to breathe the ocean air and still keep them warm on a cool night after the rains had come through. There were mostly small bungalows and small huts. Nothing fancy or too permanent. But everyone had a home. And everyone looked at each other as family. Emily thought it was a lovely community.

Katharine's trade changed every time she came back. Sometimes it was coconuts from around the world, and sometimes there were small dolls made from the women on Haiti. The small area of land sits to the east of the straight between Haiti and Puerto Rico. That area is a passageway for many sailors. During months of calm weather, the town receives many visitors.

Katharine had a lighthouse built here to help her and the other pirates with safe passage through the area. In addition to the pirates, many ships from around the globe, including England and Spain, had all made safe journeys through this area. Many years ago, when Katharine and Elsie became friends, they began to learn much about each other's way of life. Elsie taught Katharine how to communicate by telepathy and bouncing her thoughts. And Katharine taught Elsie how to be a pirate.

That morning, Emily and Madican were walking around the shops trying to find something new that Katharine had brought back.

"I hope she found some chalk and some more empty books." Emily's sentence trailed off as she began looking down the row of shops hoping to see something that looked like a leather journal.

It didn't matter to Madican that Emily often stopped speaking because she was concentrating on something. He would just read her mind and know what she was trying to get across. That day, he knew what she was looking for. Emily liked to draw. Specifically, she liked to draw Madican and Bew. Since her journal was almost full, she was looking for a new one.

But Madican had already thought of that. Emily's birthday was coming up soon and he wanted to get her something special. He had already talked to Katharine about bringing home another journal and she had agreed it would be a lovely gift. So, Katharine had pretended not to have any journals on this trip. No matter how hard Emily looked through the shops, she wouldn't find one. Madican had to work hard at not letting Emily know his secret. She could read his mind better than most Land Runners.

"Emily, Pearl wants you to look for some flour." Madican tried to change Emily's focus.

"Flour?" Emily answered. She turned and went the other way along the row of shops with Madican at her heals.

"Slow down," he insisted, halfway teasing. He knew if she had her mind set on something it would be hard to redirect her.

She slowed her pace and let him walk next to her. He resisted the urge to hold her hand. She looked so pretty that day. Her hair was up in

TIDELINES

a bun, but it had come lose and was about to fall out because she had been walking so fast. She wore a brown dress with a white apron over it. The apron had been stained from blueberries that had come in the previous week. She had tried to make a blueberry pie for Madican, but made more of a mess than a pie. Her feet were bare, like usual. She looked very plain except for her eyes. They were so beautiful and blue that to him they were the jewel that made her stand out. Every day, she wore the bracelet he gave her. He had brought her many things over the years, but that seemed to be her favorite. He thought it looked amazing on her.

She looked at him as if to say *I can read your thoughts you know*. He blushed and turned away from her walking toward a small shop with wooden bowls. She giggled and followed him.

Madican liked to see the wooden items Katharine would bring back. Under the ocean, wood eventually deteriorates, so the Swimmers didn't use it to make things as the Land Runners did. Madican's sense of curiosity and thirst for knowledge was a trait Emily truly admired. She loved to watch him learn something new about the Land Runners. It delighted her to see him study and then suddenly come to realize something special about an object.

Emily stayed back slightly while she watched him pick up bowl after bowl and investigate it. He'd feel it. Then he'd smell it. He'd hold it out as if he was weighing it in his hand. He'd stare at the object then start to laugh, knowing he had just been made aware of this new thing. Then, he'd simply put it down and move on to the next new thing.

She truly enjoyed him. They truly enjoyed each other.

I CAN READ YOUR THOUTHTS, YOU KNOW

Chapter Nine:
It Was Safer That Way

Later that day, Pearl was walking the edge of the city when she noticed a large ship heading toward the island. Katharine's second ship, the *Billie Jean*, was due back today, but this didn't look like her ship at all. The masts were much taller. And a Spanish flag was being flown. Spanish ships had been through here before, but not recently. Spain had a weak hold on the territory known as Florida in the Americas. And lately, according to Katharine's close friend Jean Lafitte, they were losing their grip fast.

Jean was quite fond of the American philosophy of independence and freedom, so he had sworn to never attack an American ship. But he did have a bad habit of attacking Spanish ships. Their booty would be sold in New Orleans and in many large Southern cities for much less than normal traders, allowing the impoverished areas to have items that were usually only afforded by the wealthy. Jean considered himself an entrepreneur helping the economic future of the Americas. He knew well that the Spanish government was about to officially lose that area to the Americas, and he enjoyed watching them lose.

Jean had visited the Isle of Bryce many times before, often bringing fine gifts to Katharine. Pearl would sneer at him, knowing that if he truly loved Katharine he would know that gold and silver was not the way to her heart. Nonetheless she knew Katharine had a fondness for him. Although she really couldn't figure out why.

When she saw the Spanish flag, Pearl was immediately on edge. She closed her eyes and turned toward the ocean. "Elsie. Elsie, can you hear me?" She waited for a response.

"Pearl?" The voice was as clear in her head as if she was standing next to her talking. "There's a large ship coming near the island. It looks like a Spanish war ship. We've not had them visit this year. Do you think you could listen?" No response. Pearl knew Elsie was trying to read their thoughts. Five minutes went by. Pearl waited.

"Pearl?"

"Yes, I'm here."

"I can't pick up on anyone, they're going too fast. When they get closer to shore they'll slow down and I'll try again. But, Pearl, they're coming in real fast. I think they want to surprise you."

Pearl turned back and headed for the tavern. At the first house she stopped and let Brett know to sound the unknown alarm. There were three alarms—known, unknown, and safe. "Known" was two bells and it was for any danger headed their way that they knew for sure was real danger. If they heard this alarm, it was every man for himself. Just get out of the town, take everything you can, and don't come back. A known enemy would destroy the town and everyone in it. It would be best to get yourself out and away from the danger. "Safe" was three bells and it was for any known friend. Jean Lafitte and Johnny Longskull were known friends and they frequented the island. Longskull liked his rum and his visits with Bew and Pearl, and Jean just liked Katharine.

An "unknown" was just one bell and it was for any potential danger. This was for a new pirate ship, a new country ship, or anyone who was showing up unannounced that was not already considered a friend or a foe. This was a reminder that all Swimmers head back to the safety of the water and a reminder that all residents of the island were sworn to secrecy.

"Mad, it's the alarm!" exclaimed Emily. The pair had been shopping in the market when she heard the bell. She had heard this type of alarm many times before. And every time it meant the same thing—he had to go. If someone saw him they might distinguish how different he was and then they would try to substantiate the rumors. Yes, there were lots of rumors. Many ships' crews questioned them about mermaids. The tales were out there amongst sailors. They had all heard stories about the friends from the water Katharine allowed to live on her island. But no one ever gave away the secret. No matter how much rum they had to drink, and no matter how much money they were offered, no one on the island or on Katharine's ship had ever confessed to knowing a Swimmer.

Emily often wondered why they felt inclined to keep the secret. After all, some were offered pots of gold for any information. But Pearl would explain that the gift of the friendship with the Swimmers was worth

IT WAS SAFER THAT WAY

more than any gold could pay. They all knew if the secret got out it could destroy all the Swimmers. And no one wanted to take that risk. Katharine was careful who she let live on her island. Only those she truly trusted could stay. If the powers of the Swimmers were harnessed then whoever controlled that power could control the oceans and all the waters of the world, and potentially could control the world.

"Okay, I'll go find Bew and head for the water. Let me know when they're gone," Madican answered as he made his way back toward the shore.

Emily made her way back to Jesse's where she hoped Pearl would meet her. Several people were trying to gather up the pigs and goats to take them into hiding in the deep brush of the jungle. Meat was important for survival on the island. And they could not risk a stranger trying to take off with all of it. Katharine had many hiding places in caves on the island. There she kept most of the provisions such as rum and silks, coffee, sugar, and wax. It was important to keep most hidden so if they were robbed, the thieves would only take what they could find in the shops, thinking that's all there was. Everyone was bustling around trying to make themselves look poorer than what they were. Hopefully this Spanish ship would take pity on them and think of them as only a small trading town, not a profitable hideout for a successful female pirate and her friends from the water.

Emily found Pearl and others at Jesse's Place. "What can I do, Pearl?" she asked.

"Well, child, don't do much of nothing right now. Just do what a barmaid does—serve food and drinks. Did Mad and Bew make it to the water?" she asked while packing up the coffee.

"I think so. He was walking that way looking for Bew." She pointed to the other side of the island.

They waited for a while before the ship made it to the dock. A group of men, led by Brett, went to the dock to greet them. Brett was one of Katharine's first residents on the island. He had been running from a lot of painful memories and found his way there. His face was oval with a sharp nose and piercing eyes. His head was smooth and bald but he kept a small beard. He had been a handsome man at some point in his life but his eyes were now clouded and sad. His features seemed to reflect the permanent scar on his soul.

TIDELINES

Brett studied the arrogance of the Lieutenant as he sent his men down to the dock to make their introductions before the captain would depart the ship. Brett was extremely intuitive to other people. He had a gift of reading people's emotions and slight actions that told him whether they were telling the truth or not. This made him the best greeter to new "unknown" visitors, and Katharine's main confidante for advice on whether or not to allow a new resident to live on the island. The soldier walking toward him was working to walk with perfect posture—a move only a truly confident man could pull off. Brett knew right away this soldier did not believe in his duty and was hesitant to even be there.

Nonetheless, the soldier approached Brett and announced himself. "I am Lieutenant Rodrigo Dominguez of the Naval Ships of Spain. My captain is Captain Juan Garcia. We understand there is a trading post here and the captain would like to come ashore to rest and possibly trade." The man breathed a sigh of relief at having expressed all his captain had asked him too. But it was obvious to Brett that he was holding something back.

"Don't believe him. They are here because they are looking for us." A voice spoke to Brett in his thoughts. He knew this voice but it had not spoken to him with such intent like this before. However, he knew to heed her warning, and he proceeded with caution.

"Welcome to the Isle of Bryce. This is our humble home and we are honored to have a member of the Spanish Navy come ashore. Please let us welcome him," Brett said slyly. He bowed slightly but kept his head raised. He wondered if the good Dominguez would even realize this action was a sign of disrespect in other parts of the world. "No, he has no idea," said Elsie's voice again. This made Brett grin.

"Thank you for your hospitality and your loyalty to the throne of Spain. I will bring the captain now." Dominguez waived at a younger soldier behind him who shuffled off immediately to fetch the captain.

"Lieutenant Dominguez, may I take you to the tavern?" Brett offered. The Lieutenant nodded in agreement and along with two other officers, followed Brett up the path toward to town.

The town sat not far from the shore behind a large dune that protected it from heavy storms. The trek to the town was not too treacherous but longer than Dominguez had hoped it would be. Once they made their way into the heart of the city, they were met by the residents who pretended to be impoverished. They didn't move around much, and

IT WAS SAFER THAT WAY

were wearing old tattered shawls. They frowned at the Lieutenant as he passed them, careful not to look at him in the face as they made their way to the tavern.

"May I present Pearl, the proprietor of Jesse's Place," Brett said as they entered the bar.

Pearl made her way toward the lieutenant. She looked him up and down without a smile. Then she blurted out "What kind of getup is that?" She had already heard from Elsie and Samuel, and knew exactly what these men were after. Pearl knew she had the element of surprise. Emily watched from the back room.

Dominguez stared at her in shock, not knowing what to think of this old lady.

"I'm just messing with you!" Pearl let out an old crazy lady laugh.

Dominguez grinned and attempted to snicker at the woman's attempt at a joke. "Well, if you must know, this is actually the finest wool garment from Spain. Only the highest-ranking officers are issued this type of uniform." He stuttered in response trying to keep his snobby nose in the air. Pearl was still half-way laughing when she stopped, looked him straight in the face and said, "Yeah, I don't care. What do you want to drink?" Emily snickered from the back room.

Dominguez found a table with three chairs and proceeded to have one of his officers wipe it off for him, and even pull out his chair. The tavern was open on two sides, like most of the homes on the island. It had long sheer drapes that hung along the roofline and blocked the sun. But today, Pearl had taken them down. They were silk from China and looked too rich to hang in an old tavern. The back area, where Emily was hiding, was for supplies and two small cots.

The younger officers did not sit down until Dominguez found the right seat for himself. After trying three different chairs, he chose the one that faced both the overhangs of the patio and the bar. Brett figured this was to make sure the Lieutenant could see the captain coming, and make sure to address the bar if need be. Brett could see that Dominguez took his title very seriously, but the man didn't have any remorse about making the younger, more inexperienced officers work for him. Brett thought this showed that Dominguez had some self-esteem issues if he had to be constantly reminded of his rank by making those in a lesser rank work so hard for him.

TIDELINES

Pearl was pouring drinks for the men when she heard some commotion outside the tavern. As the tavern was open on two sides, hearing things outside in the shops was not hard to do. Dominguez heard it too and became quietly fixed on the tall lean figure in red coming through the town. "The captain is coming," he said to his men. Brett noticed a slight quivering in Dominguez's voice.

Pearl stood at the end of the bar and watched too. Elsie was yelling at her in her head. Samuel was too. Pearl was trying to respond that it was all right, but she struggled with letting them hear her thoughts unless she was actually thinking out loud, which meant talking. Emily was watching from the back and making sure they had enough supplies for the men. She knew she may have to run into the jungle soon if too many of them came ashore. That was always tricky because you could be followed.

Emily's pictures were also hidden in the depths of the jungle. She had found a cave one day when she got lost trying to find one of Katharine's supply caves. Emily had kept that a secret. She had traded some rum for some paper one day and started drawing pictures of Madican and Bew. Their hair was hard to draw because it was so different, but Emily had a special way of drawing it that made them come to life. She mostly drew pictures of them swimming under water, something she had never seen in person. Her drawings were strictly her imagination, and her impression of the stories he told her. Madican had offered to take her swimming but she was afraid of the water. Her drawings were her way of escaping the nightmares she still had, and forgetting about the world out there that she desperately wanted to see. She knew she would be stuck on the island forever. She loved Pearl and Bew and Mad and all the people on the island. But there was a whole world out there that was calling her. For now, her drawings answered that call. There was no way she was letting some Spaniard get hold of them.

"Welcome to Jesse's," bellowed Pearl when the captain ducked under the overhang to come into the area of the bar where the tables were. He seemed to try to ignore the bellowing from an old woman and looked around the room for his Lieutenant. He found Dominguez standing next to his table and started walking toward him, completely ignoring Pearl. "Here, sir. I had it cleaned off for you," Dominguez said to the captain.

Brett thought Dominguez looked like a puppy who had just gotten in trouble and now had its tail between its legs. "Let me have the barmaid get you a drink," the lieutenant begged. The captain nodded. Dominguez

IT WAS SAFER THAT WAY

waived toward Pearl as if to say *Go on now, go get the captain a cold beverage.* Pearl rolled her eyes and shook her head but proceeded to the back for more mugs.

Brett approached the captain. "Welcome to the Isle of Bryce, sir." The captain didn't move or acknowledge him. Turning to the small crowd, Dominguez introduced his captain. "May I present Captain Juan Garcia."

Brett decided to begin the conversation. "What brings you to these waters? We hear tell that the land known as Florida, full of Spanish influence, is being taken over by the Patriots of the Americas. If you are here, that must mean the rumors are not true. For surely a captain as official as yourself would never let that territory fall back into the hands of those young Patriots." That got his attention.

"What?" The captain answered. Brett knew he had hit a nerve, but that was okay if he was opening up some communication. "I'll have you know Spain has no intention of losing that territory to the Patriots. We have a rightful claim to that area and we will not let some young *attempt at a country* take it away from us! You are mistaken. Spain is still a strong presence in Florida. You have no idea what you're talking about," he huffed.

"Forgive me, sir. I am just an islander and don't know about all that. We just know the reputation of the Spanish Navy precedes its visit to our humble home. There are stories that the Spanish Navy is the greatest in the world." Brett saw the captain sit up a little straighter and he knew he had him. "Tell us how many ships are in your command, Captain." Sitting up even a little straighter now. Was that a slight smile?

"Well, I have the honor bestowed to me by the King himself of commanding ten different ships. Dominguez here has been honored by being able to escort me this far south on our way to Puerto Rico." The captain explained. *Yep*, Brett thought to himself, *I've got him right where I want him now.*

"We would be glad to help by keeping the beacon light going tonight. If only we had some oil to spare," Brett suggested.

"We can provide you with enough oil, if you can provide my men with a good meal and good drink tonight."

"Of course," Brett answered and waived toward Pearl.

"Great," Emily thought, "now I'm going to have to go find some ham."

TIDELINES

Chapter Ten:
Lights and Eyelashes

Pearl made sure dinner was amazing and filling. Her secret recipe ensured the men would get a bit sleepy and she knew if they got sleepy they might tell her more about why they were there.

Emily tried to help wherever she could. She offered more food to those whose plates started getting empty, and she kept the mugs full. During the evening she noticed one of the men was not drinking. She made her way toward him and asked if he wanted anything else to drink. "No, thank you," he answered.

"Well, your shipmates don't seem to mind the taste of rum."

"It's not that. I'll drink a pint when I can, but tonight I have to make sure their drunken tongues don't rattle off too much." Emily wondered what they would rattle off about if given the chance. He smiled at her, wondering to himself if she would sit and talk with him. He thought she was very pretty, but not pretentious. So many women he'd meet would try to talk with him hoping for some gold from other lands, or hoping for the right to marry into a better class than theirs. He wanted to marry for love, but just hadn't found the right person yet.

"And just what kind of question should one ask that would tempt a tongue to rattle off, sir?" she questioned. He smiled back at her attempt at being sly. He was too smart for that. He was smarter than the others, which was why he chose not to drink a pint that night. "Oh, you know, we don't want to give up all our strategies when it comes to defending the good name of the King." She smiled back. She liked the way he looked at her. He was warm and unassuming. Almost genuine and not arrogant.

"So, how did you come to live on this island?" He was trying to look into her eyes. The question took her off guard. It was not an easy answer.

"My family was killed." She looked down, breaking off his gaze. "Their ship went down. I survived and Brett found me and brought me here." That question had never come up before. She hoped Brett would stick to the story.

"Seems like a nice place." His response seemed to question her honesty. He glanced around as he said it as if to convince himself it really was a nice place.

"It's my home now. How'd you come to join the King's Navy?" she asked, eager to change the subject.

"Well, it was my duty. I turned eighteen last year and I wanted to serve my country. And see the world."

"So, have you seen it?"

"Not all of it. Not yet."

"I'm sure it's exciting," she said, noting that she sounded like she was flirting.

"Yes, it can be," he answered with a bit of confidence.

"How many places have you been to?"

"Oh, too many to count. All have their own unique beauty and culture. It's really a nice job," he smiled, as if trying to convince himself.

A job? She thought. Strange choice of words. Most sailors were forced into their country's military for hopes of a better class status. Not many chose that line of "work" and not many referred to it as a job.

She stared at him for a moment. He seemed sincere as he recounted the different people and places he had visited. She could tell he really enjoyed traveling and experiencing different things. She almost felt a twinge of guilt for trying to get him to talk. He was really a nice-looking soldier. So what if she wanted to carry on a conversation?

The two talked for a while and it became obvious to the others, when their pints were low, that Emily was concentrating on his every word.

"Emily, I need a hand." Pearl thought it best to break this up.

"Okay." Emily got up from the table where she had made herself comfortable next to the young soldier and started toward Pearl.

"My name is Ethan," he stammered.

"Emily." She held out her hand.

"I'm so very glad to have met you, Emily." He smiled at her eyes. She just looked down and walked away, not sure what she was thinking about that.

TIDELINES

"Em, I need you to go get some chickens. Looks like they will stay the night and will expect to be fed in the morning." Pearl's tone was a bit strong.

"Okay." Emily responded, wondering why Pearl sounded so harsh.

Pearl picked up on Emily's questioning tone and explained, "Look, I don't think it's a good idea to make friendly with a soldier. A nice pirate, well, that's one Katharine can approve of, but not a soldier. Can't trust a soldier." Pearl shook her head. "But a pirate, well, they never lie"

Emily laughed to herself at Pearl's attempt to be convincing. But she decided it best to heed her warning and take the safe path and go find some chickens.

The Isle of Bryce was a good-sized island with plenty of hiding places. Emily thought about checking out her drawings but didn't want to risk being followed and her hiding spot being found. At night, it was easy to follow people through the thick jungle-type vegetation. She made a straight line to the caves that were about half a mile from Jesse's. It would be where Brett would have sent the people of their town to hide the livestock. There were caves that didn't go anywhere. An animal couldn't get too lost there. Most of the townspeople who kept hogs and chickens kept them near the caves most of the time anyway. With the constant visitors to the island, it was easier to keep them hidden.

Emily saw a light in the distance close to where the caves were. That was strange. All townspeople were to keep all lights out in fear of the visitors finding them. Emily picked up her pace to try to catch up with the light, which seemed to be a small lantern. It moved in quick jerks back and forth, often disappearing behind something large for a moment, only to appear again in a brief glimmer. The movement fascinated Emily as she crept closer. Soon she began to see an outline of a man that looked like he was dressed in a suit. This wasn't good. This was a Spanish soldier out roaming around the island. She knew he must be up to no good. This was too far to wander just to relieve himself. She realized he must be looking for extra supplies Katharine had hidden away from the town. Someone must have let him know about her rum.

Emily knew she had to stop him and get him back to Jesse's. It was late and she had seen some of the soldiers making their way back down to their ship for the night. Others would stay on the island in people's homes, or on hammocks on the beach. This one must have wandered off in hopes of finding something to make his captain proud. She knew

LIGHTS AND EYELASHES

she had to do something. The only thing she could think of might be a bit risky but it was all she had. Emily let out a loud blood-curdling scream. Not once, but twice.

She heard responses. People hollered for her. She heard Pearl. "Emily!" Oh, she hadn't thought about that. Pearl would be so frightened.

"Mad, can you hear me?" She sent her thoughts to her friend.

"Are you okay?" he answered.

"Yes, please tell Pearl I'm okay…. I'm near the caves and saw a soldier with a lantern…I think he is looking for the caves and I'm trying to draw him away from them"

Emily waited for Madican to answer her. She turned toward the light in the distance. It was still, as if he had stopped and was thinking about something. Suddenly it started moving. Had it heard her? This time it was coming in her direction. Thank goodness she had made the light turn around. But now what?

"Emily, Pearl is okay but she is still coming to look for you. I don't think she's very happy so you'd better have a good story."

Emily quickly rubbed some dirt on her hands and elbows. She made a small tear in the bottom of her skirt, and loosened her hair knot for good measure. She plopped herself on the ground and waited to be rescued. She turned toward the light and tried to gauge how far it was, but she had lost sight of it. When she turned back around, she saw Ethan leading two other men up the path. Her stomach flipped at the sight of him coming to rescue her.

"Emily!" he hollered for her.

"I'm here!" she answered, adding a slight bit of anguish in her voice, secretly hoping he had come alone.

He knelt down next to her. "Are you hurt?"

"Yes, I think I've hurt my ankle" she pretended to try to faint.

"Oh, well you screamed as if someone was trying to kill you."

Oh yeah, she thought to herself

"I was walking this path like I always do at night and I saw a ghost-like figure lurking in the woods." *Hmmm. Maybe that was a bit much.* But when Emily told a story she just didn't know when to stop. "It was so ugly, it looked like it was coming for me so I screamed and turned to run away. That's when I stepped on a rock or something and fell."

She looked straight into his eyes. "But, thank goodness you're here," she said, eyelashes batting. Ethan picked up Emily to carry her back and immediately felt the cold metal of her bracelet on his neck. "What is that?" he questioned.

"You mean my bracelet?"

"Yes," He pulled her arm around in front of his face to see what the cold essence was coming from. "That's a bit fancy for an island barmaid isn't it?" he said sarcastically. He recognized this piece of jewelry as being from the *Atocha*. He knew why they were here on the island and after meeting Emily he had hoped his captain was wrong. But after seeing the bracelet he knew they must be in the right place.

And Emily knew too. But she had forgotten to hide it! She knew better than to wear that in front of strangers. The rule for all the islanders was to pretend you were poor. Now she could have ruined everything. *Quick, think of something,* she thought. "This belonged to my mother. It's all I have of her," she sobbed, hiding her face in his chest and pulling her arm back around. She tried her best to be convincing.

Everyone made their way back up the path to the tavern. Realizing he may not get a real explanation from Emily, he continued back up the path with her in his arms.

Chapter Eleven:
A Grim Reminder

Juan Garcia crawled to his bed at one of the local's homes after too much rum that night. The crew tried to insist he make his way back to the ship for the night but the captain refused, saying he didn't want to be rude to the islanders by refusing their hospitality. Which was news to the islanders because they didn't recall offering up any of their beds for the night. The ship's crew seemed accustomed to this behavior and helped guide him to his makeshift bed, like a border collie herding a lost sheep. Finally, just after midnight he passed out snoring and the others found spots on the floor or right outside the house to sit down and try to sleep as well.

Pearl and Emily had long gone to sleep. They both slept in the back of the tavern. It was safer that way. Elsie and Samuel were nearby along with Madican and other Swimmers but they decided to send Bew further out as a precaution.

Elsie had been reading what Garcia was thinking and it wasn't good. She heard him discussing the rumors of Swimmers and knew he'd be looking for evidence on the island. He was not successful as a captain for the Spanish fleet and wanted to earn respect from the King of Spain. The government of Spain had lost control of Florida and was desperately trying to maintain rights to that area. Garcia knew there had been a fleet of twenty-eight Spanish ships lost at sea in the early 1600s. He knew the King prized the items on the *Atocha,* the last of the train of ships.

And if he could find that treasure, the King would be more than pleased. He may even make him Governor of the state of Florida. Since title and money were extremely important to Garcia, he had made it his life's work to find that treasure. Recently he had heard rumors of mermaids in the waters near Haiti. Unknown to his crew, he had defected from the Spanish Navy to search for the treasure. But first he needed to find the mermaids. If he could force the mermaids to show them where the treasure was, he'd be a very wealthy and successful man.

About a half mile off the coast, Elsie and Samuel were swimming in the moonlight. They were nervous and felt this was worse than other occasions when the island had been visited by ships looking for mermaids. The islanders would all keep quiet and no proof was ever given up. Most ship captains left discouraged. But this captain was different. This one was ruthless.

"This scares me," Samuel spoke to Elsie.

"I know," Elsie assured him. Samuel was a good husband and a protective father. But long ago he had agreed to let Elsie take him and their two kids to the island on one condition. It could not interfere with the Swimmers' community and secrecy. The council had not yet agreed it was time to announce themselves to the Land Runners. And Samuel did not want to violate that. The council had agreed to let them visit with Katharine on the island. They thought it would be a good start. But they didn't know how many people were actually on the island, or how many people were actually on Katharine's crews.

Samuel had said that at the first sign of trouble they had to leave. Even if that meant Elsie had to end her friendship with Katharine. Elsie had agreed but didn't think it would ever be a problem. After Katharine had rescued her they developed a strong friendship. They had become like sisters. They were always together. Katharine would take Elsie with her whenever she went in search of ships. Elsie would show Katharine where the ships were sailing. She had insight from the different flows of the schools of fish. They would change patterns based on the weather and the influences on the water, such as a large fleet of ships.

Elsie didn't like the harsh way some of the crew would take over another ship. But like Jean Lafitte and Kay Lee, Katharine only tried to take from those who already had too much, and gave to those who had little. Katharine would show Elsie all the treasures she would take. Most she took home to supply her island and some she would give to Jean for his people in New Orleans and the southern states. And the very rare special pieces she would leave to the ghosts in the ocean. Elsie and Katharine enjoyed each other and loved learning about the world they lived in. Their relationship was important to them both.

"Maybe it's time we stop visiting the island, Elsie."

A GRIM REMINDER

"Don't say that" Elsie said slowly. She knew he was probably right. It really did put Bew and Madican in harm's way. And if these Spanish people found out about them it could mean the end of all the Swimmers. She felt this Spanish captain would exploit them and treat them as pets, or worse. It reminded her of Grim Blacktoad and how close she had come to becoming a sideshow attraction. "Let's find Bew and Mad and make sure they are okay. Then I'll talk to Katharine and Pearl in the morning."

Ethan heard the snoring as he approached the hanging curtains. The moon was bright in the sky and he could clearly make out the bungalows and its surroundings. The people of the island had let Garcia stay on the outdoor patio of the largest house on the island. It was very small as far as houses go, but very grand for an island such as this. Ethan noted there were only two rooms in the little place, and neither had more than a small bed and a three-legged wooden table. The windows were more like doorways to the open air outside. They had tattered clothes for shade curtains. There was nothing remotely rich or wealthy about this island and the people on it.

He knew Emily had to have lied about the origins of the bracelet. It was not likely a small child could have kept up with it when the ship her family was traveling on had gone down. And he knew if she flaunted it around these people as much as she did around him, someone would have stolen it. After all, he knew it was worth a fortune. Ethan had been shown drawings of the inventory of lost items from the *Atocha*, and this bracelet matched the drawing perfectly. It had to have been from the *Atocha*, and there was only one way she could be in possession of it. A mermaid had to have given it to her! Ethan was excited to tell Garcia his news.

He crept past the ship's crewmen who were slumped against the walls and palm trees, anywhere they could get comfortable, trying to sleep. He needed to wake up Garcia and tell him his news. As he entered the room he smelled an ungodly stench that made him gag. Apparently, Garcia had eaten something that disagreed with him for dinner. Holding his nose and his mouth, Ethan backed out of the room and decided he'd make Garcia aware of his information over breakfast, if he could stomach it.

Chapter Twelve:
J L

Pearl was an early riser and was never around when Emily awoke. But that morning Emily awoke to see the backside of Pearl as she was peering out into Jesse's Place from the privacy of their back room. She must have heard Emily move, and she turned toward her. "Shush, darlin', I'm trying to listen."

Emily eased her way to Pearl's side so she could peek out. In the middle of all the tables sat Garcia and Ethan. Garcia was listening intently to something Ethan was trying to explain. Although Garcia liked to have his pints, he usually didn't sleep much. He and Ethan probably had been up for a bit. For someone to be up earlier than Pearl it must mean they were determined to get their day started and begin whatever mission they were on. Pearl could tell the two meant business. And she was intent on finding out more of that business. Emily closed her eyes and tried to concentrate, but she couldn't hear them. But never underestimate the hearing of an old woman who was determined to know your business.

Pearl suddenly turned and glared at Emily. "Did you let those soldiers see your bracelet?" There was fear in her question.

Emily flinched and grabbed her wrist. The bracelet was still there on her arm. "I... uh..." she didn't know what to say. Yes, Ethan had seen it the night before and she made up a story about it. Surely he would believe it?

"Child, I don't think he believes your story. He is telling Garcia that the rumors about the mermaids are true. That they are here and that you know them."

"Oh, no! No! No!" Emily shook her head in a panic. "What does that mean? What are they going to do? I'm so foolish." Emily looked down, trying to make sense of what Pearl just said. This was not good. This was against everything Katharine expected of them on the island. They all had to hide their wealth when visitors came, not flaunt it. This could ruin their relationship with the Swimmers for good. She tried to convince herself that Garcia wouldn't believe it.

"We'll see what they do, with what they think they know," Pearl said. "What exactly did you tell that young soldier last night?"

"I told him it was my mother's bracelet."

Pearl stared at the ceiling trying to think.

"Okay, this is what we're going to do. We're going to confirm that story this morning." She paused for a breath. "Get some food together for their breakfast and while we're serving them their plates I'll mention the bracelet and how we're all pleased to not hide it in front of the honorable Spanish captain and you can mention again how it was your mother's."

"Yes, and I'll tell a story about how she gave it to me, and how special it is and how she had gotten it from someone else." Emily agreed and tried to convince herself that by helping with this story, it would make her big mistake all go away.

"Okay, that's good. We must let the others know so they can confirm the story. Go out the back and fetch something to put together for these soldiers. I will head down to Brett's and talk to him."

Emily quietly got up and snuck out the back of the small room. Her emotions were numb. *How could she have been so stupid?* She knew the rules Katharine had, yet she had been so caught up in the handsome soldier and the mysterious light in the woods that she had forgotten the most important thing. And this wasn't just about letting the soldiers know they had wealth, this was letting the soldiers know about their most prized secret—the Swimmers. She had to fix this or their friends could be in danger.

She followed her path down the slope past the deepest part of the woods and jungle where the hidden caves were. She decided to fetch some ham so she took the path to the west that curved around the hill and opened up to a hidden beach. This area was special to her. It was where she hid her drawings. Not many islanders knew she had them. It was as much a therapeutic exercise for her as running with Madican was. She knew she didn't have time to draw right now, but wanted to check on them to make sure the light she saw last night had not found them.

She slowed her pace and tried to look over her shoulder to make sure no one had followed her. The cave on the hidden beach was known only to her and Madican. She assumed no one on the island knew it existed and she wanted to keep it that way. She stopped and listened for footsteps or leaves rustling. It was very quiet for the morning. Usually some of the island birds were singing by now. But at least she knew she was alone, so she cautiously approached the entrance covered by thick vines. Pushing the vines aside, she squeezed into the opening that was only as wide as she was.

But once inside, there was room to walk around. She just couldn't see anything. She felt her way to the notch in the side of the cave where she had hidden her book. Thankfully it was still there. The book was a large leather-bound collection of yellow pages. She had drawn on most of them and knew she would need to trade for another book soon. She decided it was safe to leave it so she placed it back in the notch and slipped out the same way she came in.

Almost immediately, she stopped dead in her tracks. A small fishing vessel was beached aground, about fifty yards from her. The wood was bleached and on the side of the boat was the writing JL. Why didn't she see it before? Was she really that unfocused? There didn't seem to be anyone around, so she started walking casually back to the path of the woods she had come out of. As soon as she got to the edge of the path she turned again to make sure no one was looking and when she was sure no one was there she started running up the path. The sun was rising so she knew she needed to go quickly and get the ham for breakfast. She was so focused on finding the right path, that she didn't see the eyes watching her from the woods on the other side of the cave entrances.

J L

Chapter Thirteen:
Stone Streets, Ghosts, and Gardens

By the time Emily had made her way back up to Jesse's tavern she had forgotten about the small vessel she had seen. She was nervous as she started to serve the plates to the hungry soldiers and Garcia. He kept watching her and was smiling to himself as if he knew a secret about her. She didn't like the way his stares wouldn't waiver. No matter how many times she pretended not to see him, or looked him directly in the eye, he kept staring. Smiling. Contemplating and conspiring. She wished Mad was here, but Garcia would surely tell Mad was a Swimmer if he was looking for mermaids. It was a dangerous thought.

Pearl had put up one of the many curtains that normally hung along the side of Jesse's Place and shaded the patrons from the sun. But this morning they were burlap and not silk. Emily noticed Brett coming up the packed sandy street. His steps were quick and Emily knew he must have been told about her slip-up. Hopefully he was here to help. When he approached the overhang of Jesse's Place his eyes caught hers and he gave her a look of disappointment she had never seen before. Her heart sank, knowing she had let everyone down. She turned away from his glance, hoping Garcia would not see it.

Brett knew he had to get the soldiers off the island as soon as possible. He boldly walked into Jesse's Place and announced, "Good morning, gentlemen."

Garcia took notice and looked up. He smiled at Brett and motioned for him to join him and Ethan at his table. Brett thought Garcia had taken a liking to him and thought him to be in charge of the things on the island, since he was a man. *Oh, how little he must know.* Brett snickered to himself.

"Good morning, Brett. I must say I have found your island most welcoming and I am grateful for its hospitality." He looked at Emily. She turned around and walked into the back room. It seemed the only place to shake his stare.

Brett grinned and answered the compliment. "Your visit honors us and we have been pleased to attend to you and your men. You have a hearty crew that I'm sure serves you well." Brett leaned in as if to keep others from hearing. "You are quite the leader, sir. I don't know any other ship that has sailed through here whose crew is as loyal. That only speaks to how great a captain you must be." He nodded and winked at Garcia, as if that was their little joke. Garcia was looking at him, and smiled a very proud smile.

"Well, I believe if you treat a man fairly he will work hard and until death for you." Garcia explained. Brett smiled in agreement. He wanted Garcia to feel complimented and it was working. He needed to take his mind off the mermaids.

"So where will the King's Navy be taking your crew today, sir?" Brett asked.

The captain was pleased to talk about the King. "Oh, well, the King has entrusted myself to a great task that you will understand could be a detriment to our crew if the specifics of our next voyage were shared." Garcia smiled smugly.

"Of course, forgive me for being so bold. I merely hoped to converse about your adventures and the far-off places only a loyal captain such as yourself would be entrusted with." Brett saw the captain's eyebrows raise as if he contemplated discussing the far-off places with Brett. "Our small island has such poor souls we would delight in hearing you tell us about your favorite place. Surely that would not compromise your mission, sir?"

As if on cue, several islanders along with Pearl, began to lean in and move closer to the captain's table as if he was going to tell a lavishly entertaining story. The captain saw the attention and hesitated for just a moment, not sure what he would talk about. Brett knew he had him again. It was almost too easy.

"Well, I suppose the place I enjoyed traveling to the most was Key Vacas," he started.

Almost immediately, and also as if on cue, Pearl spoke up. "Oh Emily!" she yelled to the back room. "Emily, come quick, Captain Garcia is

STONE STREETS, GHOSTS, AND GARDENS

about to tell us about his travels to Key Vacas. That's where you're from, darling!"

Emily heard this from the back and realized what the two were doing. She picked up the act and bounded to the front of the tavern pretending to be eager to hear. When she got close to the captain she said, "Oh, please tell me about that town, sir. I left with my family when I was only three years old." She played up on the sad little girl role now and hung her head. "Our ship went down and my family all drowned. A pirate ship found me floating in the wreckage. They took pity on me and brought me here to live with Pearl. This is all I have left of my family." She held out her wrist with the bracelet for everyone in the tavern to see. Some of the islanders knew the story they needed to stick to, but some didn't know yet and were shocked to see Emily share the beautiful one-of-a-kind bracelet with a stranger. Their look of shock didn't slip past Ethan.

"Your mother gave you that, right?" Ethan asked.

Emily was slightly shocked to hear him speak up that he remembered. She smiled and looked at the bracelet, then she held it to her heart for full affect. "Yes, this was a gift for my third birthday."

"Must have been very large for your wrist when you were only three."

Emily bristled and knew the argument was just starting. She had to stay calm and stick to the story. It was the only way to keep Garcia from pursuing the Swimmers and destroying their relationship. Ethan needed to catch her in a lie so he could prove to the captain these islanders were hiding mermaids. They both had a lot to gain by winning this argument.

"Yes, it was too large then so I wore it around my ankle."

Then Pearl chimed in "That's right, child, you was about ten years old when I told you to take that off from around your foot and start wearing it like a lady on your wrist, the way your mama must've wanted you to." She smiled like she was reminiscing, but really, she knew she had just dealt a blow to Ethan's argument.

Garcia was wide mouthed and not sure what to believe. Ethan too had gone quiet. Emily, with the help of Pearl, had made her point. *Now, if only he'll believe it.*

Brett saw the tension in the air and Garcia's inability to pick up on anything so he knew he had to jump on it. "Captain, please, tell us about Key Vacas."

Emily sat down and listened to Garcia tell about the pirates that lived there, the stone streets, and the large bodies of coral that made up the land there. He also told her about the beautiful gardens that bloomed practically year-round and the ghosts that wandered the streets and the cemeteries.

He was really an amazing story teller and although Emily thought she probably really wasn't from Key Vacas, he made her feel as though she wanted to visit. There was something familiar in his stories that she was able to see in her mind when he said *stone streets, ghosts, and gardens*. It was a comforting, yet confusing familiarity. She shook it off and tried not to acknowledge the deep stares coming from Ethan.

Later that day, after his ship had been readied for sailing, the captain decided to head out. He expressed they would be leaving to complete the "secret mission" the King had assigned to him. As Brett and the others watched the large vessel pull away from the dock, he tried to fight off the feeling the captain had lied to him, and that this visit was not the last they would see of Captain Garcia.

Chapter Fourteen: Jefferson and Michael

Garcia and his men had left the island two weeks ago but had not charted a specific course for anywhere. They needed to stay close enough to the Isle of Bryce to sneak back, and far enough away to be undetected. Most of the crew were beginning to wonder where the King would send them next. They hadn't been profitable on the Isle of Bryce, so surely, they would be in search of land or other ships soon. Ethan and Garcia had talked at length about the possibility, now a probability, of mermaids on that island. But their information had not been shared with the crew. It was too valuable to risk until the time was just right.

Eventually they decided on capturing a young male mermaid and force him to lead them to the *Atocha* shipwreck. Once they salvaged all the treasure they could from the wreckage, they would return to Spain with the gifts for the King, along with the mermaid. What a prize the King would receive. What gratitude Ethan and Garcia would receive!

"We must be careful about approaching the island." Ethan cautioned. "If they know we're coming they will surely hide their friends carefully."

"We will send Jefferson and Michael. They are skilled at collecting...well, let's say human cargo." Garcia smiled a weird smirk as if he already had his prize. He was so arrogant and sure of himself that it made Ethan wince.

Jefferson and Michael had been with the crew since they left Spain. The crew did not know they were not true Navy soldiers for Spain. These two men had been hired by Garcia prior to setting sail. Jefferson had a scar on his head that kept any hair from growing, but it was never sunburned. And Michael was a hefty man with one eye. The two kept to themselves when it came to the crew but Garcia didn't care. He was just glad to have some tough men on his deck.

Garcia's ship was staying about three miles off the coast of the Isle of Bryce. They did not want to alert anyone to their presence. Jefferson and Michael took a small dingy and rowed their way silently to the other side of the island from the small town they had visited before. The small vessel seemed quieter at night as it traveled across the ocean toward the island. It was a long way to row but the two men knew what they had to do. And Garcia wanted them back in three days. That didn't give them a lot of time, especially since they'd never captured a mermaid before. They thought mermaids lived in the water so they didn't quite understand why they were being told to capture one on land.

They pulled the boat ashore at the cove Ethan had described. It was very quiet and there were no signs of life anywhere. Silently, they pulled the boat across the sand and into the vines that grew along the edge of the dense foliage. Michael motioned to Jefferson to grab some palms and cover their tracks that led out of the water into the jungle. The moon was not bright that night so it was hard to see. Without a word, they made their way east toward the light they'd seen from the water as they approached the island. They knew this must be where the small village was. They were told they could find a mermaid there. Their plan was to spy on the townspeople to see where the mermaids were, what they were doing and find a good time to kidnap one of the strong male ones.

Daylight was beginning to show itself as the two men were fighting sleep. They had made their way to the top of the path that led out of the jungle. Ahead was the backside of a small bungalow. That was obviously where everyone ate. It was a type of makeshift tavern.

"This will be the perfect spot to overhear people and their conversations." Michael said. They crouched down behind some bushes close to the wall of the tavern and waited. When the sun started peeking over the horizon of the ocean in the distance they heard someone start to stir in the small room in the back of the tavern. Pearl was waking. She pulled herself off her cart and started toward the front of the tavern when she stumbled on a bucket. She cursed and kicked the bucket to the corner. This shocked Jefferson and Michael from their almost-asleep state to one of more alert listening. Soon after, a young woman woke and went into the tavern with the old woman.

"Morning, sweet child. I was thinking we might do some chicken stew today. How's that sound to you?" Pearl was talking to Emily about what they would be preparing that day.

JEFFERSON AND MICHAEL

"I think Katharine would love that, Pearl."

Pearl. Yes, that was one name they were supposed to find. She would know about the mermaids. The younger woman must be Emily, the other name they were supposed to listen for. Emily made her way out back. She was headed toward their hiding place. Both men began to stiffen their backs in case they had to defend themselves if she found them. Fortunately, she turned before she got to them and made her way down a path that led into the woods.

Jefferson whispered to Michael, "You stay here and try to listen to that old lady. I'm gonna follow the girl." Michael nodded. Jefferson carefully followed Emily down the path. He had no idea where she was going but it must have something to do with chicken stew. Eventually Emily came to a clearing and Jefferson could hear the chickens clucking. Emily was having a conversation with someone who owned the chickens. He listened and heard Emily ask for three hens. She was going to the beach to meet a friend but would be back in an hour.

Jefferson continued to follow her as she made her way further down the path to the beach. He saw her stop and look around. She put her hand over her eyes as she looked out into the water. This is it. He thought to himself. And sure enough, out from the water walked a handsome young man, smiling at the young woman.

Jefferson studied Madican. He was strong and good looking. His hair was unlike anything he had ever seen! It was shiny and flowing like glass, but flexible and iridescent like a silky fish scale, and as long as his shoulders. He could tell the young man's fingers had a little webbing. Jefferson thought he probably wouldn't have noticed the webbing if he wasn't looking for it. The young man had a sleek, dark green wrap around his waist. But he had legs. This was different. All the stories he had heard were of mermaids with fish tails! But then it made sense. The mermaids were able to walk on land and probably hide among humans this way. That's why they'd never been caught.

Suddenly the prospect of being the first person to actually catch a mermaid made Jefferson nervous and excited all at the same time. Was he really doing this? He realized he needed to charge a higher price for this catch.

He watched the two friends run up and down the beach. She was much faster when she was on the dry, packed sand. And he was able to catch up when he ran in the soft wet sand. But together, along the tideline, they ran in sync. When they quit running, the two sat on the sand together and talked. Jefferson listened to their conversation about the chicken stew and what they would be doing together that day. She was going to the secret cave to draw in her book. He was going to help Brett with an underwater map of the small bay. They would meet back here after lunch to wait for someone named Katharine who would be coming home the next day. Jefferson knew what he had to do.

He started back up the path well in front of Emily so she wouldn't see him. When he came upon Michael he found him asleep. He was so frustrated that he slapped him. Michael woke with a start and realized he had fallen asleep on his watch. Jefferson was furious. Michael started to speak but Jefferson quickly put his hand over his mouth to shut him up. Jefferson quietly explained the plan to the young male mermaid that afternoon. Michael tried to break a smile under the hand of Jefferson so he loosened his grip trying to signal to be quiet at the same time.

"It is sooner than the captain expected, but we have the best opportunity this afternoon." Jefferson told Michael the mermaid would be going down that path that afternoon to meet a young lady at the beach. Along the path they could ambush him and take him to the ship. Michael agreed. After they were sure the path was clear they started down to find the best place to hide.

JEFFERSON AND MICHAEL

Chapter Fifteen:
There Was Nothing Anyone Could Do

"Bew! Glad you're here, darlin'! You know what day it is right?" Pearl grinned at Bew, who had popped in to the tavern to say hello and help herself to the chicken stew.

"Is today Emily's birthday?" Bew squealed. She loved birthdays. The Land Runners celebrated every chance they got and to Bew that was delightful. And Pearl always celebrated with chocolate pie. Bew was only six years old but had already been able to celebrate a couple of her own birthdays with Pearl since coming to visit the island. Bew loved Emily like a big sister and couldn't wait to celebrate with her.

"Guess what Mad is giving Emily?" Bew taunted Pearl with a question she didn't think Pearl would know the answer too.

Pearl pretended she didn't already know. "I have no idea. What is it?"

"He got Katharine to find him a new drawing journal to give her!" It was Bew's idea that Madican get Emily a new drawing journal, and Bew knew Katharine would be able to find one, or get one from Jean Lafitte. Emily thought no one knew she liked to draw, but the truth was everyone knew. Bew was so excited to get to see Emily's expression. She knew Emily would be surprised.

All morning, Bew helped Pearl clean up around Jesse's Place. She straightened chairs and washed dishes. She even found some flowers to decorate the tables with. Everyone on the island celebrated birthdays. After leaving wherever they came from and starting a new life on the Isle of Bryce, it was a way to remember where they came from and who they were. Bew knew everyone would be coming to Emily's party.

Bew loved being around the islanders so much and she was so glad her mother let her visit daily. Pearl was a grandmotherly figure to her, something she didn't have under the ocean. This world on land was so different, yet Bew was fascinated by every part of it.

On the other side of town, Madican and Brett were mapping out the reefs under the sea just inside their cove. Brett hoped Madican could help them find fish and shellfish that would help supplement the food on the island. The two had become good friends over the years. Brett was like an older brother to Madican, showing him the way the Land Runners lived. They shared stories of where Brett had come from and all the places Madican had visited. Brett sensed a lot of hesitation in Madican being on the island. He could tell that being amongst the Land Runners made Mad nervous at times. It had been a long time since Katharine had brought anyone to live on this island for good. Actually, Brett thought, the last permanent resident was probably Emily.

Madican and Emily had become fast friends and Brett thought their friendship was healthy for both of them. Brett had come to the island after fleeing the New Orleans area like Pearl. In the big city, children were always running in the streets with their friends. Some were playing games and some were looking for food. Brett had always had a special place in his heart for children. He had always wanted a child of his own, but didn't think that would ever happen. He was thirty-five now and he knew he was getting older and the likelihood of meeting a wife on this island was slim. But he loved his life there and all the people he had grown close too. Pearl and Emily were his family now. And since Mad and Bew had been visiting regularly, well, they were family too.

"So, what are you planning to get for Emily for her birthday, Mad?" Brett smiled.

Mad looked up from his paper and thought for a moment on how to explain it. "Well, Emily loves to draw, you know. And Bew told me that her drawing journal is almost full. So, I arranged for Katharine to bring home a new one for her."

Brett was surprised by Madican's sincerity and the thoughtful idea he'd had. As he listened to Madican talk about Emily's upcoming birthday party he slowly began to realize that Mad was in love with Emily. And he believed the feeling was mutual. It never occurred to him that Mad would do something so genuinely sweet and thoughtful. Emily would be very happy.

Brett sat down with his hands on his knees and shook his head. The whole island was fearful, and yet kind of happy, for Mad and Emily to

THERE WAS NOTHING ANYONE COULD DO

fall in love. "Mad, I think that's the nicest thing I've ever heard anyone do for another person." Brett slowly brought his gaze to Madican.

Madican looked back at Brett, not sure why he thought that was such a big deal. It was just a drawing journal. But Mad knew how much Emily would like it and it made him feel good to think about doing something so special for her. He smiled a sheepish grin. "Yeah, I know."

Brett decided they needed to have a talk about a Swimmer and a Land Runner's relationship.

"Mad, I know you and Emily have a special friendship," Brett said. "And I think the love you have for each other is nice."

Madican sat down now too. Scared of where this was going. "Have you two ever talked about other Swimmer girls that you might know?"

What a weird question, Madican thought. "Um. No. Not really."

"Well, it might be a good idea for you to think about spending some time in the ocean with your family and meeting some nice girls."

"Oh, are you trying to tell me that I need to start courting? Like Land Runners do?" Madican was almost laughing.

"Well, maybe. How do you find a wife under water?"

"*Wife?* Wait a minute. I don't want a wife yet. I'm only sixteen."

"I know. I know. All I meant was that you needed to find someone you could think about marrying. Emily is a nice girl, but a Swimmer and a Land Runner shouldn't marry. You know that, Mad."

Madican looked away. He did not like where this was going, and Brett could tell he had hit a nerve. Elsie and Samuel had often told him of relationships in the past but all of them ended on a bad note because the families couldn't handle the differences. Of course, Emily's family was the island. And Mad's family was Elsie and Samuel and they all already knew and respected each other. If it was going to work out, these two were the ones it was going to work out with. But Pearl and Katharine and Elsie and Samuel had said for a long time that it would not be a good idea. So, Brett thought it best to discourage it.

"Brett, do you believe in love?" Mad asked before Brett could speak.

"Yes, but…"

"So do I." Madican started. "And Emily is my best friend who I love dearly. I can't imagine not having her in my life. If I married a Swimmer I'd never see Emily again. And I just can't do that." Madican's voice was quivering. "I'd rather not get married at all if it meant I couldn't see her again."

TIDELINES

Brett knew it was too late. Madican had fallen in love and there was nothing anyone could do.

"Mad, we just want the two of you to be happy. If that's with each other, then so be it. But your parents have seen relationships not work out, and no one wants either of you to get hurt." Brett tried to rationalize it.

"I know everyone loves us. But, really, neither of us is thinking about the future. We're just glad to be friends right now. And I hope that never changes." Madican got up. "I need to head back up to Jesse's Place to help with the birthday celebration. You coming?" Madican didn't want to admit he was supposed to meet Emily at the beach again.

Brett decided that Mad had ended the conversation for a reason. So he followed his lead for now and decided to try to talk to him another time.

Back at Jesse's Place, Pearl was stirring the chicken stew. She began to look around for Emily to make sure she had not come up to the tavern too early and ruin the surprise. After her run with Madican that morning, Emily had brought the chickens up for Pearl to start preparing. Then Emily said she was going to the beach for a bit. Pearl knew she would be drawing and that would keep her occupied for a while. But she wanted to make sure Emily didn't come back before everyone arrived.

It was Emily's sixteenth birthday, and Pearl wanted it to be special. They had been friends since Emily was three and Katharine had brought her to the island. Pearl was the authority figure and taught Emily how to read and write, and gave her a history lesson every now and then. Pearl wanted to make sure that Emily was smart and could handle herself if she ever had to go back to the Americas. Pearl was feeling a bit sentimental that day for some reason and sensed she needed to show Emily how much she loved her. The plan was to gather the Islanders right before she knew Emily would be coming back up to the tavern. When she arrived, they'd all yell "Surprise!" and Emily would be thrilled.

She looked out through the shades that hung along the open-air sides of the tavern and saw Madican and Brett walking toward her. She smiled at the warmth that Brett brought to a room and was glad he was joining them. Behind them, several of the islanders had started making their way to the tavern.

"Bew!" Pearl hollered looking around for her. Bew was very curious and often wandered off to find some new Land Runner things on the island. That usually meant she was visiting with an islander.

THERE WAS NOTHING ANYONE COULD DO

"Yes, Pearl." Bew popped out from the back room.

"Child, I need you to help with the most important part of this celebration."

Bew beamed and straightened her back and stuck out her chest. Finally, a responsibility fit for an adult. "Anything!" she beamed.

"In about an hour, I'm going to need you to go down to the beach where you'll find Emily. Keep her there for a bit. Don't let her come back up here just yet. When it's time, I'll send Madican to get you. Okay?"

"Ok!" Bew giggled uncontrollably, excited to take an important part in the Land Runners' celebration.

Chapter Sixteen: Daydreams

Emily sat on the same rock when she drew. It was a large rock that had a smooth surface. She could position her rear and her feet just right so the drawing book sat in her lap at a perfect angle. She faced the edge of the jungle where it met the sand. That day she was thinking about Madican and their run that morning. He looked especially handsome that day and she was thinking how it felt to hold his hand. He had held her hand that morning when they got up to leave. He held it while they walked a few feet together. She wasn't sure what that meant, but she liked the feeling of him being nice to her, and close to her. Nicer to her than any other girl. Not that there were any other girls on the island. There were a few other children, just not their age.

Emily was using one of the last few pages in her journal to draw a picture of her and Madican. Most of her drawings were of Mad and Bew, but today she felt as if she needed to draw her and Madican holding hands. They were running down the beach along the tideline, hand in hand. Her bracelet was shining in the sun and his stare was only on her. The drawing came to life quickly. It was easy for her to let the chalk flow over the paper. It was as if the drawing was drawing itself. She had the image in her mind and it just began to appear on the page.

Emily finished her work and began to daydream. She was daydreaming when she noticed something brown and bulky just inside the vines through the jungle. With the commotion of the Spanish captain's visit the other day, she had forgotten to tell Pearl about the vessel she had seen. She wondered if this was the small vessel again. She pretended to stretch and inconspicuously looked around to see if she could see anyone watching her. When she didn't see anyone, she hopped off the rock and started walking toward the vessel.

Peering through the vines she saw a small boat. It was not the same one she saw two weeks ago. This one was all wooden and dirty. And still wet! Whoever had been on that boat was still somewhere on that island. She needed to warn the others and start looking for them. She decided to be smart about it and go up a different path back toward the tavern, one that only a few people knew about. That way the stranger was not likely to see her.

Chapter Seventeen:
Johnny Longskull Has a Heart

Bew was usually very careful. Her parents allowed her to visit the island to learn as much as she could about the Land Runners. Elsie felt that someday soon the Land Runners and the Swimmers would coexist and she wanted to make sure her family was prepared. When she and Katharine became friends, Elsie knew she could trust Katharine's islanders to keep a secret and look out for Bew while she was there. She could even trust Longskull.

Bew loved coming to the island. She loved spending time with Emily and Pearl. Elsie knew they looked out for her, but she also made sure Bew was careful. She cautioned her every chance she got to make sure Bew was looking over her shoulder and heeding Pearl's warnings when necessary. When Pearl said head for the water, that's where Bew was supposed to go. No questions asked. And Bew was good about following the rules.

But today she was too excited to be cautious. She was going to help with the celebration! She had done all the chores that Pearl had asked her to do. She was fidgety and wanted to go get Emily as soon as possible. But Pearl had said it wasn't time yet. She sulked at the bar while she sipped on some water. Longskull was at the other end and saw her looking sullen.

"Hey girl," he said to her from across the way. She looked up and smiled at him, hoping he might have a job she could do. Instead he made a funny face. She laughed a deep belly laugh that made Longskull smile. His crew thought he came to visit the island for the rum. But the truth was he just enjoyed his time with Bew and Pearl. Pearl always had a special plate of food for him, anything he asked for. And he wasn't picky. Chicken or pork were his favorites. And Bew made him smile. He loved the way her innocent smile and deep solid laughter seemed sincerely focused on him. He had spent his life being the tough pirate that everyone feared. It was a sweet soft feeling to be loved by a little girl, one so genuine. He had forgotten how it felt to be loved, but Bew made him realize that there was still good in the world, still people who saw through the years of thievery and the rough beards, people who didn't mind the sword at his side or the dirt under his nails. He was loved unconditionally by this little girl and it just made his heart melt. But he would never show it.

"Come here and give your old Longskull a hug, girl." He growled at her under his smile. She continued to giggle but made her way to him and hugged his neck tight. Every time she did this he caught a tear in his eye. She jumped down and immediately began telling him about Emily's birthday and Madican's gift and the food Pearl was preparing. She could go on and on for hours. But he just took it all in. He noticed Pearl watching him out of the corner of his eye and it made him proud to have her approve of his friendship with Bew. Bew liked to hear his stories and she liked to tell him tales too.

"So where did you go this week, Johnny?" She was the only one who was allowed to call him by his first name.

"Well, girl, this week my crew and I made our way around the edge of Haiti. We found an abandoned town with gold streets and silver trees." His eyes widened at the idea. Bew smiled but looked at him as if she didn't believe him.

"Where are you going next week?" she teased him.

"I am going on another adventure, of course. But this time, it's to the Keys off the coast of Florida to search for sunken treasure ships filled with jewels!" He loved to embellish.

"But Captain Longskull, sir," she put on the air of a wealthy woman, "how will you ever fulfill your task this time?" She moved her hand as if to waive a fan in front of her face trying not to smile at her silliness.

"I was a captain once, I can be a captain again!" he cheered and raised his glass.

Bew pretended to faint in delight, while Longskull's crew hollered and raised their glasses too. The two laughed and laughed at their silliness.

"Okay, Bew, it's time to go get Emily," Pearl spoke over the noise.

Bew hopped down off Longskull's lap and started to run, but she suddenly stopped. She turned and made her way back to the old man.

TIDELINES

"See you soon," she said and hugged his neck again, this time leaving a small kiss on his wasteland of a cheek. Then she ran away toward the jungle path. Longskull touched his cheek and was silent.

Bew made her way down the path to find Emily, as Pearl had told her to do. The path was on a slope most of the way. Some parts were rocky and some were almost covered in vines. She had to watch her step but she wanted to move fast. Her heart was pounding and she was grinning from ear to ear. That day she was not watching the woods like her mother had cautioned her. When she slowed to part some vines that had grown over the path she was hit on the head from behind. She never saw it coming.

JOHNNY LONGSKULL HAS A HEART

PART THREE:

LAND RUNNERS VS SWIMMERS

Chapter Eighteen:
Oops

"Are you crazy?" Michael almost screamed but he knew islanders could hear him. "That's a little girl! *Not* a young man!"

By now, Jefferson had had just about enough of the bullying from Michael. He didn't care if it was a boy or a girl. It was a mermaid and that's all that mattered. "It's a mermaid!" he answered. "Who cares if it's a boy or a girl?"

"I'll tell you who will care—the captain. He specifically said the young male mermaid. He knows something about a treasure and the captain intends on using that."

"Well, maybe this girl knows something too."

"Check to see if she is breathing. You knocked her out cold, you idiot."

"Yeah, she's still alive."

After a few choice words, the two men decided to pick up the girl and take her with them. If they left her she would just tell everyone anyway and then they won't have a chance to even get the young male. Their best option, they decided, was just to take her and hope the captain could use her instead.

When Swimmers and Land Runners sleep they can't communicate telepathically. Their subconscious takes over and blocks anyone from trying to get in or out. So, when Jefferson and Michael hit Bew on the head, it was probably in their best interest because she had no way to scream out. And they would be gone before anyone knew she was missing. They made it to the main ship with Bew wrapped in a dark cloth. Once aboard, the captain could tell they were less than excited to be back to present him with their capture. The captain and Ethan stood over the wrapped body and saw that it was smaller than he had expected.

When he saw the cloth start to move, he realized they'd at least brought him a living mermaid. He stared at the two men who did not look back at him.

"Gentlemen. I see you brought us a living creature." There was awkward silence. "Is it the mermaid I asked for?" He thought he would give them the benefit of the doubt.

"Yes, sir. We found the mermaid you told us to get."

The captain was suspicious and told the two to open the cloth. When they did, the captain was shocked to see a young girl bound and gagged. Her glass-like hair was unlike anything he had seen before. And her eyes, although closed, were very big. He pushed her back with his toe to see if she would move.

Slowly her eyes started to open and she began to wriggle. She tried to scream out but her mouth was covered and it obviously hurt her head to try to scream so she just lay there. Ethan saw this happening and bent down next to her. He had a slight sense of decency and realized that this young girl was very frightened. What they all didn't know was that she was desperately trying to call out to her parents and Madican. Her head was badly bruised so it was hard for her to concentrate. Ethan untied her and led her to a room that had been set up for her brother, but it had a bed where she could rest.

"This is ridiculous!" the captain yelled at the two kidnappers. "You have brought us a child! What were you thinking?"

Jefferson was quick to formulate a lie, "Well, sir, the young male had already swum off into the ocean. We overheard the two mermaids talking, and they both know where the treasure was. We figured it would be better to have one mermaid than no mermaid." He mustered an attempt at a proud smile.

Michael tried to play along, "Yes, sir, the girl knows exactly where the *Atocha* is."

Garcia was not sure whether or not he should believe the two men. But rather than let on that he was indecisive, he chose to ignore the comments from the two and simply send them to their quarters.

"Sir, you promised a reward." Jefferson opened his mouth. Garcia slowly turned toward him and reminded him that he asked for a male mermaid. The reward was not going to be paid. But since he was an honorable captain he would see to paying half the reward if the girl really knew the location of the *Atocha*. "If not, then it will be the plank for you," he promised.

The two shuddered at the thought of walking the plank and secretly prayed that the girl knew where that ship was.

OOPS

Chapter Nineteen: Definitely Defensive Now

Emily made her way up the other path toward the tavern. She was eager to tell everyone about the small vessel. But she began to remember that Madican had reminded her about her birthday. Maybe the boat belonged to someone coming to surprise her? But who? Everyone she knew lived on that island, or in the water. No, it didn't belong there. She was sure of it. As she approached the tavern she saw almost all the islanders gathering around the tables. She was about to ruin her own surprise. Pearl tried to surprise her every year so she just humored her and let her do it. She didn't want to ruin that for Pearl.

"Mad, can you hear me?" Emily closed her eyes and started talking to Madican.

"Yeah, Emily. You're supposed to be at the beach drawing in your journal. What are you doing?"

"I saw a boat hidden in the vines. I think we may have company. Is there supposed to be someone here for my party? Or should I tell Katharine about it?"

"What? No, no one is coming that isn't already here. We need to let everyone know right away. You'll have to come in and interrupt the party. Pearl will understand."

"I was afraid you'd say that. Okay."

Emily left the solace of the jungle and stepped out into the clearing next to the edge of the tavern. Almost immediately Pearl turned and looked at her. It was like she had a sixth sense or something.

"Pearl! I need to tell you something!" she spoke loud enough for Pearl to hear her and most of the islanders to turn around. "There's a small boat docked on the beach down the west path past the chickens."

Pearl seemed to hear her but she was in a daze. Emily realized that she had a look of fear and horror on her face. She made a path straight for Emily, almost knocking over three islanders. "Where's Bew?" Her voice and her whole body shook when she asked.

"I don't know. I haven't seen her." Emily was afraid to answer that question. Panic flooded her heart. She looked around thinking she would see Bew sitting on a chair in the corner or playing in the silk curtains that Pearl hung for walls. But Bew wasn't there. Pearl dropped to her knees and started crying. Madican's hands were at his temples. He was trying to concentrate on calling Bew, and his parents.

Pearl had been trying to reach Bew for ten minutes with no response. She had suspected the worse but didn't want to admit it. When Emily came into the tavern and mentioned a boat, Pearl feared someone had taken Bew. Unable to communicate with anyone, Madican ran into the jungle and down the path. Longskull stood up and drew his sword, aiming to follow Madican. Emily was trying to put it all together. She was watching Pearl on her knees crying, the other islanders looking around at each other not knowing what to do, and Longskull pointing to some men and getting ready to follow Madican. Emily began to run after Madican. Just inside the entrance to the path she caught up to him.

"Go back!" he yelled at her. She stopped in her tracks. Why would he tell her that? She wanted to help and she was going to go down that path too. She started running again. She knew where the boat would be, or was. Maybe they could find her together. Bew was important to her too.

"Emily!" Elsie's voice stopped her again. "Tell me what happened. Please," came Elsie's pleas.

Emily stopped running to answer her. "I don't know what happened. I was on the beach. Alone. I saw something through the vines just off the beach. It didn't look right so I went to it to see what it was. When I realized it was a boat, I knew I had to tell everyone that we may have visitors so I ran up the other path to the tavern."

"Did you see anyone or anything strange?" Elsie was crying.

"No." Emily didn't know what to say.

"We've been trying to call her and she isn't responding!" Now Elsie sounded hysterical.

"Maybe she is sleeping" Emily suggested, realizing how ridiculous that sounded.

Longskull had caught up to Emily and was making his way around her to catch up to Madican.

Emily waited for a response from Elsie, but when she didn't get anything she started down the path again. She saw Madican and Longskull up ahead looking at a spot where the vines grew over the path.

When she caught up to them, Madican said, "She was taken right here." He pointed to the ground.

Taken. Emily shuddered. She couldn't understand what he was trying to say. She was confused. Why would he think she was taken? Where was she supposed to be? Emily looked at an area where the ground had been stirred up. Leaves and dirt were moved around as if there had been a scuffle. For a Swimmer, Mad knew how the land worked pretty well. The knowledge he possessed astounded her sometimes. It was as if he had always been on land. He was aware of things others would overlook. Maybe it was his curiosity about the Land Runners and their way of life that kept him aware of the little details. Whatever it was, Emily was proud of him, but she didn't understand why he thought Bew was missing.

He turned toward her as if she had been speaking out loud and said, "Bew was sent down here to get you for your party. She was supposed to keep you occupied until Pearl told her to bring you up. She was supposed to be with you!" His voice suddenly sounded angry.

"Mad, I don't know anything. I never saw her." Emily couldn't help sounding defensive.

"Why did you leave? She was supposed to come to you!"

"I told you! I saw a boat that had been hidden and I knew Katharine and Pearl should know. You told me they should know." Emily was definitely defensive now.

"Why did you come up the other path? Did you see something?"

"No, I came up the other path to avoid whoever was in that boat. I had no idea Bew was coming down the west side." She was pleading now. She didn't want Mad angry at her.

Madican sat silent for a minute. Emily didn't know what else to say. She wanted to shut her eyes and make this all go away. Madican turned away from her and stared down toward the ocean. She knew he was talking to his parents.

"I have to go. My mother is trying to contact Bew and she needs me right now."

"Let's go find her, Mad." Emily was summoning her inner strength.

Madican seemed shocked to hear her say that. He quickly looked at her and said, "You need to stay here."

Emily shuddered. His words were cold and lacked the emotion she was used to. All she wanted to do was help and he was like a stone wall.

DEFINITIVELY DEFENSIVE NOW

Chapter Twenty:
Don't Confuse Guilt with Grief and Worry

Emily sat alone in what could be called the dining room of Jesse's Place. The islanders were all talking about Bew and where she could be. With Madican's report about what he had seen on the path, and Emily's reports of a strange boat, they'd concluded that she had been taken. Three hours had passed and there had not been any word from Bew. Elsie and Samuel had feared the worse, but Madican told everyone that he knew she was alive. He knew she had been taken for a reason. Someone needed her for something. They wouldn't just take her to kill her. Pearl, Brett and the islanders agreed that made sense, and it made them feel better to have hope for her safe return.

Emily watched as they debated where to look for her and how to bring her home. She felt like joining in but really had no idea what to say. She thought it was best to just watch and listen. She was keeping silent for Madican's sake too. She felt a distance between them now. He wouldn't look at her, and he wouldn't speak to her.

Elsie was hesitant to ask any other Swimmers for help. This was just the sort of thing they warned her about. This was the reason why Swimmers and Land Runners shouldn't coexist. But Elsie knew others could pick up the path a ship would have taken and be able to try to contact Bew. She felt she had no choice but to ask for help. She and Samuel would head out to deeper water to try to convince any of them she could to help her find her daughter.

Brett suggested that Longskull start out first. He should head North West. Longskull was extremely fond of Bew and would do anything for her. The old pirate may have been semi-retired from his pirating days but he could still wield a sword better than anyone else in the gulf and Caribbean waters. Elsie and Samuel would send some close friends to follow along with him so they could keep in touch.

Katharine had arrived the day of the party as a surprise for Emily's birthday. If the ship Emily saw was the one that took Bew, then it would have left out from the other side of the island to avoid Katharine's ship. Once Elsie could convince her friends in the water for help, Katharine would be heading out to follow any leads the Swimmers could give her.

Deep inside she feared a pirate crew had taken Bew, and she knew that would be a hard battle to fight if it came to it. Many of her run-ins with other pirates often turned to tales of mermaids, or Swimmers. She overheard many men say how they wished they had the magic a mermaid would bring to help them find treasure. If someone had found out about the mermaids that practically lived on her island, it wouldn't be hard for them to kidnap one to help them find a treasure. Pirates were a different breed. She had known so many throughout her life that she knew to fear them. Most were greedy and selfish, and gave no thought to another's life. They were dirty and ruthless. They did not appreciate the finer things in life. They would just as soon throw a beautiful hand carved trunk over the side of a boat if it didn't serve a purpose. They didn't see the beauty in things, only the money it could provide them.

This is what she feared for Bew. If Bew couldn't give them what they wanted, they wouldn't keep her. And for a Swimmer, tossing her over the side only meant saving her life. She knew Bew's fate would be worse. Katharine's thoughts turned to Jean Lafitte. He had an army of men who would gladly help fight. Katharine wasn't sure if she liked the thought that Jean would do anything for her. And this would mean introducing Jean to her best kept secret and she didn't know if that was what Elsie and Samuel would want. Katharine just wasn't sure she could trust him. Whenever Jean visited the Isle of Bryce, Brett had nothing good to say about him. Brett tried to convince Katharine that Jean was a liar, a manipulator, and an opportunist. Katharine thought those ideas were preposterous. Yet, she did admit that Brett had never been wrong about anyone before. She decided to wait to ask for Jean's help. Maybe only as a last resort, she convinced herself.

Emily kept watching with nothing to say. It all seemed very confusing. There was no clear plan in place yet everyone wanted to do something. Madican was talking with everyone. He seemed so calm but not really in control. Emily hoped he would look at her and ask her to

DON'T CONFUSE GUILT WITH GRIEF AND WORRY

join them and give everyone her opinions on what they should do. But he never once looked her way.

After a while Emily felt drawn to get up and check the back-west path. She wandered down the slope, lost in her thoughts. She began to feel guilty about being at the beach yesterday. If it wasn't her birthday then Pearl wouldn't have sent Bew down to find her. And she wouldn't have been kidnapped. Emily was suddenly overcome with grief and guilt and emotions that she didn't understand or like. She fell to the ground and began crying. She knew it was her fault. Her fault that Bew had been taken. She was a horrible person for this and now everyone hated her and blamed her. Everyone, especially Madican. This thought made her even more upset and she let out a mournful wail.

Right then Pearl showed up at her side. "Child, don't you blame yourself for this." *How does Pearl always know what she is thinking?*

"But it's all my fault" Emily tried to reach out for Pearl in hopes that she would take her in her big arms and hold her and rock her and make it all go away. But Pearl pulled back and shook her head. "Uh uh. You're not going to get out of this one," she said. Emily didn't know what she meant so she reached for her again. "No, ma'am. Don't you go feeling sorry for yourself. I ain't going to buy into that. You're not the reason why Bew is gone." Her voice softened a bit when she said Bew's name.

"It's my fault," Emily stated again.

"No, it ain't. You're confusing guilt with grief and worry." Pearl corrected her. Emily wiped her face on her skirt. "Little girl," Pearl started. She hadn't called Emily that in many years. It's what she used to call her after Emily first came to the island. Pearl was the only one who called her that. Emily had told her when she was six years old that she was no longer "little" and that Pearl shouldn't call her that anymore. So since then Pearl had stopped, but only to start calling her "Child."

Pearl continued, "You can't feel sorry for yourself or responsible for this. You need to focus that feeling and energy on helping find Bew." Pearl was looking deep into her eyes now. Emily was always calmer when she did that. She knew Pearl was in control and knew best when she stared into her eyes. It would almost put Emily into a trance.

"Pearl, we need to get organized about this," Emily said with new-found strength and wisdom.

"Yes, we do." Pearl smiled at her. Emily realized that she liked this new strength and control.

"I know what we need to do," Emily said.

"Okay. Let's go tell the others." Pearl was realizing Emily's new strength.

When Emily and Pearl arrived back at Jesse's Place, they found everyone listening to Madican talking under his breath. He had been communicating with Elsie and everyone was silent so he could concentrate. The two women quietly slipped into the crowd and stood behind Brett. He saw Emily sneaking up behind him and noticed right away that she had been crying. Brett sensed that she had been confused about her feelings but had come to terms with things. He put his arm around her and gave her a slight squeeze as if to say, *You're good now. Good for you.* And he leaned over and kissed her forehead. This made Emily happy. Brett was one of her favorite people and she was so pleased he approved.

"Okay. Mother has heard from Bew." Cries of relief and sighs were heard in the crowd. Emily's heart fluttered.

"She is on a ship but she isn't sure where. Her communication is broken. Mother thinks she may be injured. But she is alive." Hollers and screams and cheers rose up from Jesse's Place. But Emily noticed Madican wasn't cheering. He continued, "She is in a lot of danger because she has been out of the water for a while. She will need to get in the water soon if she is going to survive."

"Who took her?" came a question from the crowd.

"Mother isn't sure," Mad answered.

"Why did they take her? She is so young and small" another questioned.

"I don't know." Madican was feeling cornered and Emily could see he was trying to make sense of everything. She looked to Katharine who was her stoic self, standing slightly out of the crowd watching as her islanders called the shots and made decisions on what to do. This made Emily a bit angry. Katharine was supposed to be their leader and she wasn't making any decisions. But Katharine's leadership often allowed for a democratic way of doing things. She often let her crew decide which direction to take. This kept them feeling as if they could make some decisions and be in control. This kept them loyal.

But today Emily was not okay with letting them think for themselves. It was too chaotic under the circumstances. Someone needed to take control. *They are hearing that Bew is alive so they need to do something but everyone*

DON'T CONFUSE GUILT WITH GRIEF AND WORRY

kept shouting out different ideas without anyone taking charge. Emily decided *she* needed to do something. Something deep inside her took over and she stood up on a table and yelled, "Hey!"

Everyone stopped and looked at her, including Madican and Katharine. Emily suddenly realized she shouldn't have done that. Her stomach turned and she felt sick. But everyone was waiting to hear what she had to say. It was if they were longing for someone to tell them what to do. So, she gave it a go.

"Mad, has your mother had any success with getting other Swimmers to help us?"

Madican looked as if it hurt him to talk to her. "Yes, there are others willing to help. They're reluctant but willing."

"Good. Okay, here's what we're going to do." She glanced at Katharine who was smiling at her. Her arms were crossed and she had a questioning look on her face, but she was definitely smiling at her. Then she looked at Brett and Pearl, who were smiling too. Pearl gave a nod as if to say, "Go on little girl, you got this," and Brett winked a confident wink. Emily felt if she had the approval of these three she could take on anything.

"First, I need ten volunteers to go with the *Billie Jean*'s crew, with your permission of course, Katharine." Emily looked her way again and she nodded in approval. "That ship will go in search of Bew. Madican, can you arrange for a Swimmer to escort the ship so we can keep in contact with Longskull's ship? Your mother and father will be much more effective at searching for Bew if they can do it together."

"Yes, okay." Madican turned around and placed his hands to his ears to begin communicating with Elsie.

Emily continued, "Pearl will stay here to watch over the island. Brett and I will go with Katharine on *The Black Susan*. She'll sail as soon as we can load supplies. We'll follow the *Billie Jean* and any signs Samuel and Elsie can give us, but we need to be on the water ready to go and not here discussing it." She stopped for a moment to give the commands time to sink in. Everyone was shocked to see Emily in such a role. She was taking charge and it suited her.

Katharine paid attention to the feeling of the crowd. Most people seemed okay with listening to Emily and following her control, but they were used to following Katharine's direction. She knew if she was hovering around, they would want to hear from her. She decided to speak.

"You heard her. Let's go!"

The crowd started shuffling around. Brett took names of people who would be escorting Longskull and people who could help get the ships ready.

Emily looked for Madican, but he had walked away from the crowd into town.

"Child, where'd you fine that woman?" Pearl came up behind her and gave her the hug she was hoping for earlier that day.

"I don't know what came over me, Pearl," Emily said.

Katharine moved toward Emily. "Thank you, Emily. The group really needed someone to take control."

Emily was shocked at Katharine's compliment and grinned sheepishly at her. Then she remembered her mission, "Well we can't help Bew by sitting here. We need to go."

Emily watched as the crowd began falling into place. Pearl was barking orders about what supplies to pack and Brett was taking names for who would be going on which ship. Most of the men on the island had agreed to go on either Katharine's ship or on Longskull's ship. No one wanted to wait on the island, but they all agreed on who should stay behind and look after the island to keep it running like normal. The waters had been calm lately, except for this event, and there was no need to expect attacks or problems.

DON'T CONFUSE GUILT WITH GRIEF AND WORRY

Chapter Twenty-One: Spirits in the Sky

"Emily, are you coming?" Pearl hollered across the street. They were preparing to go with Katharine. Emily knew what she had to do, but it was a hard decision. She did not want to leave Pearl who had been like a mother to her. She knew Pearl would be fine, but Emily wasn't so sure about herself. She had not been on a boat since that day. "Oh, Pearl, you know I really don't want to go!" Emily's fear was overcoming her as she kicked the sandy gravel with her toe.

"Emily, you can help Katharine and the others find Bew. Mad communicates best with you, and Elsie needs you, child." Pearl put a hand on her shoulder. "I know you can do it, Em." She looked into her eyes and tried to tell her mind that all was going to be okay, but the message just didn't get out.

Emily hugged her hard and tried to imagine them seeing each other again. Pearl would make pork tenderloin and some sort of sweet chocolate and coconut desert for Bew. They just had to find her and bring her back. Emily didn't want to imagine her life without Pearl or Bew, or any of her friends. And Madican, well, she just couldn't bear that thought. At least he would be with her. He would be on the ship with her, she assured herself. What was this feeling? Did she love him? The thought of him protecting her and watching over her gave her a good feeling. She imagined him holding her hand while they boarded the ship, and letting her put her head on his lap so she could sleep while the boat rocked. These images provided so much calmness. Pearl smiled at her intently. Emily could swear she read her mind.

"Now you listen to me, child. You stay close to Mad. No matter what, you stay close to his side. Don't get into no fighting match with no pirate. You don't know the bad pirates like Katharine does. She's used to putting up her fists, you ain't." She had both hands on her shoulders now. "If you feel the boat sway or crack, you head for the water. Mad and Elsie will know what to do."

Emily stared at Pearl. She suddenly had a sense that she would never see her again. "Pearl, I…" she stammered.

"Don't say anything," Pearl insisted. "You just go do what you need to do for Bew's sake." Emily hugged Pearl tight. Looking over her shoulder she saw Brett at the dock waving at her to go. The ships were loosely tied to the poles and were pulling against them with every wave. It was as if the ships were ready to go look for Bew too.

She slowly loosened her grip on Pearl and bent down for her bag. She didn't own much, just some shirts that she would be taking with her. Emily made the decision to leave the drawings in the cave. That way she had to come back. She just had too. She didn't look at Pearl again. She wanted to remember her warm hug.

Madican was waiting at the base of the ramp. "Come on!" He yelled. She knew he was eager to go find Bew and she did not want to hold him up. Ever since Bew had been taken he had quit talking to her thoughts. She knew he blamed her in some way. He didn't look at her when she approached him.

"I'm ready," she said.

"Emily, I know this is scary for you, and I'm grateful for your help. You need to know that I am going to do everything I can to protect you." Emily's heart skipped a beat. "But if comes down to you or Bew, I hope you know what I have to do."

Emily's heart sank. Of course she knew. Make him choose between her and his sister? Of course not. She would not want to put him in that position. She knew she would have to take care of herself. For the first time, she would have to make sure nothing happened to herself. There would be no Pearl, Katharine, or even Elsie to save her. She was going to have to save herself. But hopefully it wouldn't even come to that.

She shuddered thinking about that and decided to try not to think about how scared she was.

They walked up the plank into the ship together. Thoughts of the trip with her family poured over her. She got a bit lightheaded and looked for someplace to sit down.

Madican took her by the arm and led her to a small bench. "If you sit here and watch the water you'll feel better," he told her. *But why wouldn't he look at her?*

SPIRITS IN THE SKY

Later Emily found a small area in the corner with a makeshift bed. Four hours into the trip, Madican was swimming and she was all alone. He promised to keep close to the ship in case she needed him. She looked up and saw the opening to the bow of the ship. The stars were bright but the moon was nowhere in sight. She climbed the rungs to the opening and looked out. All around were shipmates walking and talking. Everyone was hurrying but they all seemed in sync. They each had their position and their job to do. One woman, Anna, was on the crow's nest, but she was leaning over the side as if she were asleep. Another, Milo, was using a spyglass to look for other ships or any lights. Emily recognized him as the first ship's mate for *The Black Susan*.

Suddenly Katharine's silhouette appeared a few feet away. When her eyes got better accustomed to the darkness she could make out her face. She was smiling at Emily. Emily crawled out of the hole and walked toward her.

"Emily." Katharine addressed her. She was not warm in her greetings as Pearl was.

"I'm afraid I fell asleep for a bit," Emily confessed.

"That's all right," Katharine answered. "We will be out here for a while, I fear. A little rest will be good for your anxiety."

"Oh, I'm not anxious. I'm glad to be helping in any way," Emily protested.

"I'm glad to have you on board. You will be a great communicator with Mad and his family. You know I wouldn't ask if it wasn't necessary." Katharine peered into her eyes.

"I know." Emily looked down. "How many days?" Emily asked realizing Katharine had a time frame. She must know something.

"Elsie thinks Captain Garcia has her and is taking her to the *Atocha*," Katharine answered. "And that's just a few days from here."

"Why? I don't understand," Emily lied, trying to hide her bracelet with her other hand. She suddenly realized why Garcia wanted a mermaid. He wanted someone to find the sunken treasure for him. And she knew that since Ethan had seen her bracelet, they must have assumed that there were indeed mermaids on that island, or nearby. They'd taken Bew to find the treasure.

Katharine had been like a mother to Emily since she rescued her all those years ago. She was just a toddler and was traumatized from her ship sinking, but she took to Katharine immediately. She didn't know

TIDELINES

why she loved her so much. She wasn't warm like Pearl, or funny and cute like Bew. And she didn't know how to talk to her like her real mother had. But there was something about Katharine that Emily was just drawn too. She respected her and the way she made herself a woman's place in a man's world. But mostly she appreciated the fact that Katharine seemed to respect Emily too.

"What is it?" Katharine asked.

"I'm afraid Mad is upset with me. He has not been the same since Bew was taken." Emily thought she might as well get a woman's opinion.

"Oh." Katharine straightened up, a bit hesitant to involve herself in Emily's feelings for Madican. "I'm sure Madican is just worried, Em." Emily shook her head and Katharine continued. "Do you think he blames you?"

"Maybe. He was supposed to go running with me on the beach that morning. We always meet at the same spot." Emily seemed to let her gaze move toward the stars. Katharine knew that forlorn look. She often had it about Jean. Being far away from someone you love was hard. And it was easy to daydream about them.

"That morning he didn't come down. Instead, Bew came down the path he normally took. She didn't know any better." Emily started crying again. She had cried so much since Bew had been taken. She knew Bew was still alive because she could hear her. The girl was reaching out to anyone who could hear her. She was not great at the out-of-water telepathy but had been practicing.

Madican could tell that Bew was still out of the water. It had been two days and he knew she needed to get in the water. Swimmers can be out of the water for long periods of time, but just like fish their skin will begin to dry. Their whole being depends on water, just like Land Runners depend on air. They can hold their breath, but only for so long.

Emily felt broken. In her heart she knew it was her fault that Bew had been taken. She knew Madican blamed her. She was stuck on this huge scary pirate ship and she was scared she would never see Pearl again. She also knew she was going to die in a big pirate battle. But she tried to tell herself that if sacrificing her life meant Bew's return then it would be worth it. But she was still scared.

Katharine leaned in, put her arm around her and gave her a quick uncomfortable squeeze. "You'll be all right," she tried to assure her. They both sat in silence for a minute. "Well, I'm going to check on the crew,"

Katharine said. She stood up and left Emily alone. Emily looked up at the stars and tried to concentrate on Bew. She tried to call for her a few times but couldn't get an answer. She only hoped Bew could hear her.

"Elsie?" Emily called.

"I'm here" she answered.

"Have you heard from Bew?" Emily asked.

"No, but Samuel says he is trying to keep her calm. He has been trying to talk to her and tell her we're all coming for her."

Emily stopped listening for her. She didn't like thinking about little Bew so scared. She got up and decided to stretch her legs. She couldn't really run on the ship. There were no tidelines here, so she walked back and forth. It didn't do the same to calm her as running used to, but it was something. When she got tired she went to the edge of the ship and peered over the side. The water was deep green and wavy. She looked for glimpses of shimmering hair. Nothing. *They were swimming low tonight*, she thought. She looked toward the sky and saw the stars. This was usually the time of night that she and Pearl would sit on the rocks and watch for spirits in the sky, as Pearl called them. Pearl said that the spirits of their ancestors would fly around in the sky pretending to be stars and they would look down and keep them safe.

"Look there's Julie," Pearl would point to the brightest star in the sky and exclaim that was her mother. "And there's Nancy. And over there are Phillip and Simon. And there's Jacqueline and Deborah." She would name everyone. Emily thought it was funny that the names always changed. Either Pearl had a huge family, or she was full of tall tales.

But Shannon was always a shooting star. Pearl didn't elaborate on who Shannon was. But Emily thought she may have been her sister. Every time they saw a shooting star, that name was the same.

Tonight, Emily really missed their time. Pearl told her stories about the spirits when they were alive. She made up things about her family back in the Americas and all the trouble they got into. They were really a raucous bunch of people, Emily thought. They were always going to jail, or fighting someone. But Emily loved the stories, and Pearl loved to tell them.

Chapter Twenty-Two: Jean Lafitte

He stood on the edge of his balcony looking out over the water. From the observer he appeared to be deep in thought, but the reality was that he was simply contemplating what he would have for dinner. He was a quiet and still man, so he was often mistaken for being a deep thinker. Jean Lafitte was a fine dresser with deep dark wavy hair, a pointy noise, sharp cheek bones, and hazel eyes. He was often mistaken for a light-skinned black man, but he was Caucasian by race, French by culture. His aloof appearance served his persona well. His thievery provided him wealth beyond his dreams. And it provided the ability to provide supplies and luxury items to those in the Southern regions of the new Americas at a price less than even an honest man would charge.

Jean Lafitte was tall and thin. He was not special to look at but he could gaze into your eyes and make you feel as though he had left the world and entered your soul, without reservation. That idea would make you stop and question why, and stammer over your thoughts. He was soft spoken but defiant in his opinions. He had his own thoughts and didn't change them based on the whims of the few people he let into his life. He valued others' opinions but always kept his own.

His friends included the most evil of pirates and the most powerful of politicians. He was always in the presence of beautiful woman and very intelligent men. And sometimes intelligent women and beautiful men. He appreciated beauty in everything and tried to align it with the science behind it. He often wondered why some men preferred blondes and some preferred brunettes, when he fancied both. As long as they were sharp-witted.

He believed he was an entrepreneur and a hero. He robbed from the wealthy, tyrannical countries and sold to the new country of the Americas—a land full of dreams and hopes for success and individuality. He was in awe of the North American land and its people. He believed in their cause for Patriotism and was well aware that the British were not finished trying to keep those colonies for themselves. He and his brother ran a profitable pirating organization in the Gulf of Mexico. They lived most of the year in Barataria, a massive home hidden in the swampy islands south of New Orleans. They provided that area with many goods, often rare and fancy goods, for a much better price than regular traders.

His elaborate home in Barataria was filled with men and women who would have been slaves. Jean would often pick a few of the would-be slaves from the ships he captured and robbed from. He brought them to his large home to help run the place. But he paid them, and paid them well. This encouraged their loyalty. And after all, the thought of being sold into slavery was a much worse option.

He agreed on many occasions to assist in defending the Americas against the British. But his favorite past time was fighting the Spanish. They held the area of Florida, but just by a thread. They were quickly about to lose that area and he knew he could expand his trade there too. He loved attacking their ships because they were more of a challenge than the British. The British gave up too easily. But the Spanish were often seen attempting to wield their swords as they sunk to the bottom of the ocean, drowning. They never gave up.

His port was quickly becoming the largest trading colony in North America and he knew it. He knew the kind of power he had. His reputation as a fierce pirate was comical to him. He wasn't fierce, just demanding. And he was in love with Katharine the pirate. He thought about her upcoming visit. He wanted to have her with him all the time, but he knew her passion for being on the water and her need to be loyal and to provide for her ships and her island. He debated how he could spend more time with her, but he too didn't want to give up the empire-like environment he had built. Both he and Katharine were selfish in their desires but their hearts only had room for each other. Jean pretended to have many girlfriends, but his heart and true love only belonged to Katharine.

He spent many hours contemplating how he could have her all to himself, the one treasure that had eluded him. He had wealth that was measured in material items such as jewels, art and assets, but she was the one thing he had to have to complete it all.

Chapter Twenty-Three: Demons and Ghosts

Emily paced the edge of the ship trying to talk to Madican. He was swimming too far and it was making her nervous. Being on a ship for the first time since she came to the Isle of Bryce was making her nauseated. Her mind was flooded with images of her family and the water. And the darkness. She knew it had to be Elsie who had rescued her. But she never talked about it. And Elsie never brought it up either. She probably knew how upset it would make Emily to relive that experience. In some ways, Emily felt that surviving that sinking ship was a curse. She relived it daily. Every day she saw her family drown. And every day she remembered being the one who was rescued, and wished it was her who drowned instead.

She peered across the ocean and looked for any signs of Swimmers. No one was near. Emily sighed and turned around. She made her way to the crates in the bottom of the ship that held food. Maybe something to eat would take her mind off things.

Brett was eating some crackers when she came in.

"Hello, Emily," he said carefully. He could tell her mind was troubled.

Emily smiled back and said, "Are there more crackers?"

"Sure, sit down and I will get more."

"Thank you." Emily sat down and took another deep breath.

"Emily, are you feeling okay?" Brett asked.

"Not really. My stomach is a bit sick from ship moving up and down."

"Oh," Brett smiled, knowing she was not telling the whole truth. He was good that way. "How is Mad? Are the Swimmers keeping up with the ship?"

"I don't know" She didn't think she wanted to talk about it.

"Oh?" Brett questioned.

"Yeah, I've been trying to call him all morning and he won't respond. I don't think they are near. What if they can't keep up? What if we run into something and the boat starts to sink and they aren't around? What are we going to do?" Emily's breathing began to come fast. She was starting to panic. "I can't swim, Brett. Half the men on this ship can't swim! How are we going to rescue Bew if the men are all dead and I'm not here and Katharine's ship is lost and you're gone and everyone..." She trailed off, struggling to both breathe and talk as her panic became more intense.

Brett grabbed her by the shoulders. "Emily, look at me!" He shook her shoulders trying to make her focus on him. "Look at me!" Finally, her eyes met his. They were glazed over and he could tell she was extremely scared and panicked.

"Brett?" she could barely speak his name.

"Emily, listen to me. We're going to be fine. The Swimmers are near. If anything happens they will help us."

Emily slowly sat down without saying anything. Her mind was thinking of the Isle of Bryce, Jesse's Place, Pearl, her drawings, running with Mad, eating coconut with Bew. Bew. *Bew. Bew!* Suddenly she snapped back into present day and remembered why she was on the ship. She had to help rescue Bew.

"Brett!" She looked up realizing he was still right there with her. He was like an uncle to her. He hugged her tight. Not having to say anything, they both knew that for now they were okay.

After a minute Brett spoke, "Emily, your mind is scaring you. It might be best for you to rest for a bit." He eased her down on the bench so she could relax. She knew better than to fight it and let herself fall asleep. Brett was someone she could trust.

Brett went up deck and called Madican, Elsie, and Samuel. No response. He admitted to himself that he was a bit scared too. Ships were not his best friend either. When Katharine took her trips he never volunteered to go. She knew he was better suited to stay on the island and help look out for things, but she wanted him to know how much she appreciated him and the only way she knew how to do that, besides bringing him expensive gifts, was to offer to take him on her ship to see other parts of the world. He appreciated that but always declined.

TIDELINES

Except this one time. He jumped at the chance to help rescue Bew. This was not a "searching for" type of trip. They knew where she was. This was a rescue mission. He felt so close to Bew and couldn't bear losing another child. He had run away when his little girl died and found himself begging for mercy from Katharine's crew and eventually living on the Isle of Bryce. But his daughter's death still haunted him. After years with Pearl's motherly wisdom, he began to realize that no matter how far he ran, he could never run away from her death. He had to accept it. He, along with the other people on the island, had grown to love Bew and Madican. They were always around and the islanders loved teaching them about the Land Runners. They were so inquisitive and innocent. And now Bew was… Well, he couldn't think about that. He was going to help rescue her. He couldn't run from death again.

He decided to look for Katharine. She would most likely be in her cabin studying the compasses and maps to make sure they were on course. She had traveled this trip many times but always checked and double checked her maps.

Katharine's cabin was not as elegant as it could be. She had robbed more than twenty ships in her career as a pirate but never kept much for herself. A necklace every so often, or a candelabra when it was beautiful. But she chose to give most of the luxuries to her crew. The walls were wooden planks covered with silks to filter the light and offer privacy. The bedding was ample with goose down mattresses and pillows, and jewel-colored silk blankets with tassels in the corners. There were pillows all over the cot that matched the blankets in color. A wooden table took up little space in the middle of the room. It was usually covered with maps and compasses.

There was always tea. Her favorite tea pot went with her everywhere. Madican had given it to her. He said it was from the *Atocha*. Jean told her that the Spanish had probably acquired it from a rare Chinese ship making passage to the middle Americas for trade. She had several candelabras that she changed out with the seasons. A more elaborate one for the celebration of Jesus' birth, and a simpler one for the summer solstice. She had a modest collection of candelabras. She didn't keep everything she robbed, just the ones she liked.

There was a black-belted trunk with clothing for many nights. Katharine did enjoy her clothes. She felt an authoritative presence was bought with tailored, well-fitting clothes fit for a queen. But they had to be functional as well. She couldn't very well take over a Spanish ship wearing a bustle and skirt. Her blouses were sleek and attractive. Her pants were giving and moved with her legs well. She often embellished the garments with pens and jeweled ropes for her sleeves and hips and ankles. Tied tight around her neck was a black ribbon with small pearls sewn on the edges. In the middle was a pink cameo of Kay Lee. Inside the clasp cover was a flower petal that Jean had given her when they first met. She was the best-dressed pirate in the Caribbean. And she made sure Jean knew that too.

Brett knocked on her door. "Come in," she answered.

Brett made his way into the small galley that smelled like chamomile and lilacs. "Katharine, I'm sorry to bother you."

"You are never a bother, Brett," Katharine spoke softly to him. He had a hard time reading her aura. She was so stoic. All the time.

"I'm sorry, Emily is really upset. She hasn't talked to Madican today and she is very worried he is not around. I was hoping you had talked to Elsie."

"Elsie must stay connected to Bew as much as possible" she snapped, obviously upset. She was so focused that it was hard for her to think of anyone but Bew. She had to stay aware of Elsie and Samuel at all times. And she knew they were tired. "This area does not have a current that moves fast enough." There was frustration in Katharine's voice. "They are having to swim this by themselves. I am keeping the sails low so we can pace ourselves. But Elsie is not doing well." Katharine realized she had admitted that out loud and sat down in defeat.

"I thought we were getting Longskull's help?" Brett asked.

"We were. His ships would be the best way we could fight Captain Garcia and rescue Bew. But Elsie is struggling. She can't talk to me because it would take too much of her strength. Samuel is keeping me pointed in the right direction, but only by sight, not by mind. My best captain is keeping watch day and night to ensure we follow them. Samuel with dive in and out of water to let my captain know which direction to follow. That takes less energy than talking to me." She stopped and stared out her window. "I know she wants me to follow them. But I'm afraid I might need Jean's help."

"Katharine, can I suggest another option?" Brett asked.

"Quickly."

"We know they are taking her to the *Atocha*. Madican knows where that is. We can go to Jean with Madican. Send Elsie and Samuel to follow Bew and Captain Garcia to the *Atocha* wreck. As long as Bew tells them where to go they won't hurt her. She is the key to their treasure right now. They won't do anything to her. We would have time to get to Jean and get his help."

"I had thought of that but I can't bear to be away from Elsie right now. She is so distraught. She needs me. And I don't know what I'd do if something happened to Bew. It's my fault she isn't with us now anyway. If I hadn't brought Elsie back to the island and invited her family, and if I hadn't promised they would be safe…"

Katharine's voice began to quiver. She breathed in hard and tried to stop the tears from flowing down her cheek but it was to no avail. "And Jean doesn't know about the Swimmers. If that secret ever got out…" Katharine continued to cry silently.

"Oh, Katharine, you cannot blame yourself for this. This is no one's fault but Captain Garcia's. No one could have known this would happen. We all agreed to let them be a part of our island family. Knowing Bew and her family has been…" Brett paused then finished his thought out loud "…a blessing". He pictured his daughter.

Katharine looked at Brett slowly and knew what he was thinking. She reached over and hugged him tight. *What a good friend he had been.* Everyone on her island had their demons or their ghosts. They made it through the hard times by leaning on each other. They'd all had their issues so they never judged each other. They only lifted each other up and tried to support each other when the ghosts and demons came out.

DEMONS AND GHOSTS

Chapter Twenty-Four:
Salty Kisses

Emily blinked her eyes at the sun filtering through the cracks in the ceiling of the cubby hole. She had been dreaming of pork tenderloin and coconuts. She was eating the most delicious meal that Pearl had ever made. She was starving after her run with Mad and they were enjoying a huge meal together. Later she would sketch his picture in her hidden cave and then they would be going fishing for dinner. They would be celebrating Brett's birthday and they were providing the meal. Bew was running down the street with other children from the island. They were laughing and chasing the baby goats. She looked over and saw Mad watching her.

"I love to see you smile," he said softly. She was staring into his eyes. His hand met hers and he squeezed it. She felt him moving in closer to her, never losing his stare. Was this what a first kiss was like? He came closer and closer. Should she close her eyes or keep them open? This felt perfect. Just what she wanted all her life. Just what she needed. His lips met hers for a brief second as she decided to close her eyes. Then gone. He wasn't there.

She opened her eyes quickly but he was gone. No one was there. Pearl...gone. Bew...gone. Goats...gone. "No!" She screamed and jumped up from the table. Pork tenderloin...gone. She looked every direction. No sign of anyone. "Pearrrrrrrrrl!" she yelled. No one. She started running in the street. She looked down and didn't even see any footprints. Swimmers left prints with small indentions between the toes where the webbing was. She desperately looked for Bew's prints. Nothing. *Bew! Mad!* She began to sob without control. She couldn't breathe and cry at the same time. There were too many tears. They wouldn't stop. The sorrow was overwhelming. Where was everyone? She was all alone! Not okay. Not okay. Not okay. She was struggling to breathe. Tears were all over her face now, flowing into her mouth and nose.

She tried to take a breath and sucked in water. Salty tears. No air. Suddenly everything went black. A chilling horrific thought came over her. She knew this feeling. She was drowning! She tried to breathe in but kept sucking in salty tears. No, salt water. Ocean water. She was in the ocean drowning again. She was all alone. She was panicking. She looked around for Elsie. No one. It was dark. She tried to adjust her eyes and to breathe. She couldn't do either. Her chest felt heavy and her head began to hurt. Now she was sinking to the bottom. She was dying.

She suddenly jerked to the left. Something had her arm and was pulling her. Was she going up? She didn't know what was happening. This didn't feel like before. Someone held her arm tight. It was too tight. But it was being pulled to the surface. She could see light now. But she still couldn't breathe. Her lungs had filled up with her tears. The light was getting closer. Was that Mad's hair reflecting the light? Yes! He had her arm and was rushing her to the surface! *Oh, Mad!* She loved him so much! She had always known it and now he was rescuing her! Would it be in time?

She reached the surface and her head popped out of the water. She immediately saw him next to her. She opened her mouth to speak but she couldn't breathe. *Can't breathe!* Mad saw the panic in her and rushed her to the shore—their shore—on the Isle of Bryce. She was home! She was starting to drift into darkness now. She had been without air for too long and was dying. He drug her out of the water and they collapsed on the tideline. He pushed her chest to release all the water. He rolled her on her side and she spit out all the tears. She began to sputter and her tears that had filled up her lungs were making room for fresh air. She saw Mad looking at her and crying. Was she dead? Had she died? No! There was more to live. She knew now that she loved him and needed him to know that. She couldn't die without telling him that.

She fought to breathe and began to grab her chest. She coughed and began to realize that she was alive and that he had saved her because he loved her. He was telling her over and over that he loved her. She looked at him and found his eyes and knew he was speaking to her mind. She spoke back and expressed her love for him too. "I can't lose you! I won't lose you!" he cried in her thoughts. She knew her tears had cleared out of her lungs for him. The fresh air was him. Her new life was with him.

SALTY KISSES

She threw her arms around him and held him tighter than she had ever held anyone. And right there on their beach, they had their first kiss. It seemed to last forever. It was not soft, but it was not too hard. It was a kiss that was a long time coming so it didn't want to stop. But they pulled away at the same time and looked each other in the eye. They shared the same thought at the same time. "I love you."

Emily woke up when she fell off the bench. What a dream. Her lungs were sore but she thought that must be from crying so hard in her sleep. Her face was stained with salt lines. But she had so many emotions flowing through her that she wasn't sure what to think. She loved Madican. Yes! She loved Mad! And she needed him to know it. The rest of the dream scared her. Why did everyone disappear? She decided not to think about that part, that it must have been part of the emotional build-up to the kiss. Oh, the kiss. She smiled to herself and wondered if the real thing would be as nice as her dream. She wanted to talk to him more than ever now. But she didn't know if he was near or not.

Emily had a newfound sense of excitement and energy. She needed to rescue Bew and tell Mad that she loved him. In that order. Maybe. Depended on who she saw first. As she walked the deck of the ship she imagined being the one to find Bew and fighting off the bad men who were holding her captive. Emily felt as though she could take them all on. She had never wielded a sword before but how hard could it be? She could do it. She pretended to lunge forward and stab a Spaniard in the gut. Then she swung around to defend herself from the attacked from the back. Then her right! Then her left!

Katharine started clapping. She had been watching Emily's moves. "Are you ready for this, Em?" Katharine smiled at her. Emily stopped and ran up to Katharine hugging her tight around the waist.

"Katharine, I'm so glad you're here!" She smiled up at her. "I had a dream about Mad and I know what I need to do."

Katharine smiled. She knew what Emily was going to say. They all knew it. They all knew that someday Emily and Madican would realize they had strong feelings for each other and there was a good chance they could fall in love. Unfortunately, that was forbidden among Swimmers. Pearl didn't think it was such a great idea either. It had happened in the past: A Swimmer would fall in love with a Land Runner and risk everything to be together. But none had the support of a community like the

Isle of Bryce. The others had to survive on their own, always hiding each other's true identity from their families. It was not a way to live.

Katharine thought about Jean and how their worlds were so different. She had not let him know how wealthy she and her island family were. There was something in her that was not trusting of a pirate. Maybe that was because she herself was a pirate. But she always feared that he would ultimately try to destroy the island for her wealth. He had plenty of money himself, and she couldn't see how anyone could even spend that much. But, she had been around pirates all her life so she knew how they thought. And she knew pirates never had enough. It's what kept them on the water all the time. They were never satisfied with enough. They always wanted more. And deep down she knew Jean was the same way.

But Emily and Mad were different. Their love was true love and she knew it. Pearl and Brett knew it and so did Elsie and Samuel. Now Emily and Mad knew it. Katharine smiled at her Emily's happiness. Emily was like a daughter to her and she was happy to see Emily so alive with energy and enthusiasm again. She didn't know how this would all turn out, but for now it was good to have Emily happy.

"You love him" Katharine said knowingly.

"Yes," Emily answered and snuggled into Katharine a bit tighter. There was enough tightness in hugs to go around.

"Well, let's go find him." She pulled away and became stoic Katharine again. Emily smiled a knowing smile and followed her to the highest point on the ship. They looked out into the water. The sun was high in the sky so Emily calculated it to be mid-day. That was the best time to see the farthest. Katharine reached for her spyglass and looked out toward the edge of the ocean. She slowly spanned the waves. Slower and slower. She stopped. The spyglass stayed on her eye as a smile came over her mouth. Emily was excited. *Was it Mad?* She could hardly hold it in.

Katharine turned toward Emily and handed her the spyglass. She couldn't hold it in either. She was grinning from ear to ear. "He's there." She pointed to the sea and helped Emily position the spyglass. It took her a minute but she finally saw what Katharine had seen. A beautiful pod of dolphins playing in the water on the horizon, their silhouettes looking like angels against the sky when they jumped out of the water. And in the middle of them all was Madican. He was playing with the dolphins and flying in between jumps and dives with the rest. His figure came out of the water and gracefully dove back down. Over and over he did this. Every time Emily whispered "again" he would fly out of the water and spin or flip. Just for her delight. She giggled and smiled at it all. He was here. He had been here all along. He loved her. And she loved him.

Chapter Twenty-Five: Meet Me Under the Crow's Nest

The ship was not smooth that evening. The waves were stronger and caused a rocking motion that made most of the shipmates a bit queasy. "If Pearl was here she'd know what to do." Emily thought to herself. She didn't like the idea of the crew not feeling well. They were supposed to run the ship, after all. And just what would happen if they ran into trouble and the whole crew was ill! Emily didn't like the anxious feeling she got when those who were trying to take care of her weren't able to take care of themselves.

She noticed Milo, Anna, and the crew continued to try to work even though most were holding their stomachs or leaning over the side. She admired that amount of dedication. Looking around she saw Brett and Katharine hurrying back and forth from the main cabin where Katharine's room was to the opposite side of the ship. They carried bottles and small boxes that were jewel colored and seemed out of place on a huge dirty pirate ship. Emily got up and followed Brett. She almost ran into him when he hurried out of the cabin.

"Hey there," Brett smiled at Emily

"What's the hurrying about?" Emily asked. "Can I help do something?" She was hoping they'd heard something about Bew and hoped the boxes and bottles had something to do with her rescue.

"Well, sure you can help. Pearl sent some potions and herbs with Katharine that are supposed to help with sea sickness." Brett rolled his eyes at the thought of the crew having fallen ill by being at sea. How many times had they gone before and not gotten sick in waters rougher than these? "Katharine is trying to remember the right mixture to help her crew."

"Ok. Maybe I can help. Pearl showed me mixes all the time," Emily answered.

Brett looked surprised that he had not thought about that. He pointed to the smaller cabin at the end of the boat. "I think she is in that cabin working on something now."

Emily turned and walked quickly to the small cabin. She peered through the round window on the old wooden door. Inside she saw Katharine leaning over a small table covered in the boxes and bottles. She was shaking her head and running her hands through her hair. Emily had never seen her so disheveled before. Katharine was always so perfectly put together. She always had the right answer and seemed to do the right thing. To see her upset and anxious scared Emily a little. This was not the woman she thought she knew. Emily slowly opened the door, determined to come in and try to help. It was obvious that Katharine needed help to figure out the mixture and Emily was not going to let her try to figure it out all by herself. After all, she had seen Pearl do it a million times. She was sure she could replicate it.

"Katharine, Brett said I could find you here." Emily announced, unsure if she should sound happy or excited or quiet or orderly. She wanted to let Katharine know she was there and then she would figure out how to offer help without seeming to take control.

Katharine was startled when she heard Emily's voice. Katharine was not the type of woman to show weakness, especially to her crew. Her immediate expression when she looked up was sharp and angry. Until she saw Emily.

When her face softened she answered Emily. "Yes, I'm here trying to make sense of these notes that Pearl sent. The crew is starting to feel the effects of sea sickness and Pearl was good enough to send some things to help. But I'm afraid I'm just no good at this." She looked down as Emily detected a slight quiver in her voice. This must be extremely important to Katharine, she thought. And she was right. Katharine's life revolved around her crew and her island. She loved to sail so she needed a crew. The crew needed a livelihood so she paid them, well. She gave them an island to live on and they helped maintain it with the items she brought back when she pirated. And now it was in jeopardy, and she felt as if it was her fault for even bringing Elsie and her family to the island. And ….

Emily watched as Katharine's eyes began to get glossy. Emily could tell this was uncomfortable to Katharine so she stuck to the subject. "I've watched Pearl make mixes all the time. Let me help." She walked toward the little table and started looking at what Katharine had laid out. There were herbs and spices in a small bowl ready to be stirred together but no wet ingredients had been added yet. "Try adding about a spoonful from the blue bottle." Emily didn't have to coax her. Katharine quickly obeyed. Emily watched as all the ingredients mixed up into a distasteful-looking paste.

"That looks just like what it's supposed to look like," Emily announced.

"Is it ready for the crew now?" Katharine asked.

"I believe so." Emily looked at Katharine. "Let's try."

The two walked out of the cabin with the bowl of paste. Katharine started dosing it out to each crew member. It was amazing that what little was in that bowl ended up being enough for each sick person to have a spoonful. Emily watched as each crew member thanked Katharine as she treated them. They had a great deal of respect for her. Maybe this was why taking care of them was so important to her. They respected her because she really loved taking care of them and doing things for them. They worked for her and were loyal to her because she was always fair and giving. These men and women were usually running from something that was not right in their life. Katharine made life right again. Katharine gave them a family. Of course she was panicking when she was trying to make the mixture. It was important, because it was the right thing to do for her family. Emily smiled to herself at that thought. She had the same admiration and love for Katharine that the others had.

"Em." Madican broke into her thoughts.

"Mad!" Emily thought back.

"I'm coming aboard. Where are you?" he asked.

"Under the crow's nest."

Emily listened for any movement on the outside of the ship. If he was climbing aboard, he would need ropes and wooden slats for leverage to climb. She was certain she would hear some bit of commotion. But there was nothing. Suddenly, she saw him. Across the deck, on the other side of the ship, he leapt over the side onto the ship. He shook off the water that was dripping from his hair and the green wrap around his hips. She really liked looking at him. As if he read her mind, he looked at her and caught her eyes. He smiled a silly smile and then started walking toward her. They both had the same thought.

His pace picked up a bit, and then so did hers. She felt as if she couldn't get to him fast enough.

He wanted to hold her so badly. He had missed her terribly. He knew he had made her suffer, thinking he was angry with her. He was overcome with anguish. He needed to be with her again, not against her. He had realized that if they were going to find Bew, they could only do it together.

They were almost running when she fell into him. His arms held her as she threw her hands around his neck. Without hesitation, their lips met. Emily felt as if she was in another world. And he was so happy to be with her again. The kiss was soft and special, but over quickly. They each had so much they wanted to say. But they didn't let go. When they looked at each other they couldn't stop holding each other. They knew they were where they were supposed to be.

"Well, I was wondering when you two were going to figure that out." It was Steven, one of Katharine's best ship mates. He smiled as he walked by them, nudging Madican in the side with his elbow. Madican jerked as it tickled his side. Emily giggled and loosened her grip. The two kept staring at each other until Katharine walked up.

"Welcome back, Madican." She was her normal, distant self again. "I hope you two lovebirds remember that we have work to do." Leave it to Katharine to snap them back to reality.

Madican looked down, breaking their stare. "Emily, I owe you an apology."

Emily wanted to stop him. She knew it was hard on him when Bew was taken. But it was hard on her too. She wanted to know what he was going to say, so she didn't stop him. Instead, she lifted his chin so he could look at her again and met his eyes with a smile.

"I know it isn't your fault, Em." He squeaked it out. He had struggled with blaming Emily for what happened, but he knew he was wrong. Emily was not at fault. And here she was on a ship, her greatest nightmare, trying to help find Bew and bring her home.

Emily hugged him and tried to reassure him. "We're going to find her."

As Katharine watched, she knew it was best to let Madican apologize and let the two work it out. She knew there was work to be done and she needed Madican and Emily to work together if they had any luck of finding Bew. But now that the two had kissed and made up, it was time to get back to work.

"Madican."

"Yes, ma'am," he answered, dropping Emily's hug. Emily complied and stood next to him.

"What is the latest from your mother?" Katharine asked.

"She said that Captain Garcia's ship was spotted by some Swimmers off the coast of Florida near Key West. They talked to Bew and she is alive but very dry." Madican's voice cracked when he said this. For a Swimmer to be dry meant they'd been without water for too long. If they didn't get into the water soon, it was not good. He knew the possible outcomes and knew Captain Garcia probably didn't know that she needed water. He shook off his fears and continued with the stiffness of a soldier. "The Swimmers attempted to contact Garcia and begged him to release Bew or to at least let her get in the water. They tried to convince him that she needed water and without it she wouldn't be any good to him anyway." His voice cracked again, but he continued. "The Swimmers believe Garcia thinks the voices in his head are demons. He doesn't know that we can talk to him in his head. The Swimmers are trying to convince Bew to help show him by talking to him, but she is very weak." Madican stopped.

Katharine could tell he was done talking about it for now. It was upsetting. But she needed to ask one more question. "Any news from Longskull's ship?"

Madican was silent for a moment then answered. "No. I'm sorry."

Chapter Twenty-Six:
Help Is on the Horizon

The view of the sea from the side of a pirate ship compares to nothing else on earth. The sun, or moon depending on the time of day, can look as if you could reach out and pinch it. The surface of the water glistens and the waves hypnotize you as they form a train of white caps on the horizon. Your eyes play tricks on you as you try to distinguish a dolphin's fin from a wave. When you close your eyes, you can hear the sound of seagulls calling to each other while flying over a shadow of anchovies being herded by sharks from below. That day, Emily was taking it all in. She was concentrating on the beauty of her natural surroundings while trying to forget that she was on a ship, something she'd had nightmares about since she was three. She was amazed at how strong she felt and how her fear had seemed to subside since being on this ship. She had a mission—to rescue Bew. And no amount of fear was going to stop her.

She was staring at the horizon looking for dolphins when she noticed three tiny triangular forms on the edge of the ocean. *Ships.* In the middle of the ocean that could mean anyone. Emily knew they were expecting help from Longskull, but as far as she knew, he only had one ship. Emily alerted the nearest crew member who already seemed to be aware of the ships. He smiled and put his spyglass away when she excitedly told him the news.

She felt a bit helpless as she noticed all the crew members hastening to their positions. If the three ships were not friendly, the crew knew they must be ready. *The Black Susan* was a fast ship. Some say it was the fastest ship in the Caribbean. But it was still hard to outrun another pirate ship. And if they were government ships that could be worse. Both Spain and England had bounties on pirate heads. The pirate ships had historically caused problems by attacking and robbing traveling cargo ships and soldiering ships. So, any citizen who could prove they killed a known pirate would be paid handsomely. This is something all pirates feared. Over the last fifty years, pirating had started to slow down because of this bounty. It used to be that no one fought back. It was easy to plunder a ship. But when a ship's crew knew they could make money, lots of money, by killing a pirate, well, they started fighting back.

Emily watched as the ships slowly came into view. She was relieved to see the three familiar flags. The first ship was the *Billie Jean*, Katharine's ship. Her flag was a deep navy blue with a pale green image of a palm tree in the middle. The tree represented a lone island in the middle of the deep blue sea. She sailed for her island and the people she called family.

The other two ships were Longskull's. They were *Caesar's Ghost* and *Hector's Grip*. His flags were taller than they were long. It was a different type of flag. After all, Longskull was a different type of pirate. He never followed the rules that were agreed on by all pirates, and that meant his flag had to be different too. It hung long instead of wide, with the image of an elongated skull wrapped in a snake on the black cloth. Emily had asked him about the skull when she was only five. He told her a long skull made people think he was smart because he must have a bigger brain. He wanted to scare his enemies by making them think he was really smart. This made her laugh to herself because that wasn't very scary, and his head was normal shaped.

That night Longskull and some of his crew met with Katharine and Brett on *The Black Susan*. Katharine had filled him in on what they knew. Longskull was angrier than Katharine had ever seen him. He was quiet when they all recalled how Bew had been captured, but his face got redder and redder. His brow wrinkled and his back hunched as if he could push off away from the table and jump up at any moment. The true pirate in him was showing.

"From my calculations we seem to be two days away from where Madican says the *Atocha* is located. We think that they have already made it there and are trying to persuade Bew to start bringing up the treasure." Longskull began breathing like a mad bull. Most pirates didn't have a problem killing people. But Longskull was like Katharine and didn't like to do that. That was probably why they were good friends and she allowed him to frequent her island. He pirated because it was really all he knew how to do, but he never killed anyone unless his life was in danger.

HELP IS ON THE HORIZON

But he would not hesitate to kill anyone who hurt Bew. The anger inside him was welling up.

"So what's the plan?" Longskull asked.

"We didn't want to make any definite plans until we had all our ships together, Johnny." Katharine sat down at her table. "Now that you're here, we can put our heads together and come up with a plan." Her soft voice was keeping Longskull from any quick and unplanned reactions, like jumping off the ship and trying to swim there in an effort to get there as fast as he could. Brett had told Katharine how to be soothing with her words and that it would keep the bull of a man calmer and allow them to think smart about how to proceed.

"Madican says the *Atocha* is located in a bay. This is a great place for Garcia to hide his ship while they try to bring up the treasure." Katharine watched Longskull's face for a reaction. Brett nodded for her to continue. "This is also a great place for us to surprise him."

"Well, it looks like we've got four ships to one, right?" Longskull began calculating now.

"That's right. I figure we'll send two ships in to surprise him and keep two ships out of the bay just beyond the breakers in case he is able to make a run for it." Katharine suggested.

"Be assured, he won't have a chance to run for it," Longskull promised.

Katharine shuddered slightly at this. She didn't want to have to kill anyone. She just wanted to get Bew and get out of there fast. But she knew what a battle might come to. It would not be easy. She thought about Emily and Madican, and Brett, and wondered if they would have what it took if it came down to it.

Chapter Twenty-Seven: Fear the Swarm of Mermaids

"Captain, the girl is ready to talk" Ethan had been on the ship with Garcia and Bew. He had watched Bew's progress over the past several days and knew she was declining in health. He assumed she needed water, but the poor girl wouldn't speak. She was defiant and stubborn. A trait he actually admired. Ethan had felt a bit of guilt when Michael and Jefferson had arrived with her rather than a young male mermaid.

"Good. Bring her to me," Garcia ordered.

"Sir, she is in a bad state and can't walk." Ethan stumbled over his words a bit. The crew had been telling Garcia that she was not doing well but he thought it was a scheme to get him to let her in the water. Now he was faced with a mermaid who was going to die rather than get his treasure and Ethan didn't know how he would respond to that.

Garcia stood up. He had been on this ship too long and he was tired and angry and anxious to get to that treasure. They had made it to the Keys, where the ship was rumored to have gone down. But only this girl knew where it was. "I don't care if you have to carry her. I said bring her to me," he said with clinched teeth.

Ethan left, and soon returned carrying Bew. Her coloring had gone pale and her limbs were limp. Her hair had lost its shine and she couldn't open her eyes or speak. This time, Ethan was not as respectful of the captain. "Here she is. She is about to die. She must have water if you want her to do any work for you." He looked straight at the captain whose jaw had dropped. He did not realize the girl had gotten so sick. He had been stupid for not listening to his crew, but he couldn't let them know that. He couldn't let them see any weakness in judgment on his part. He couldn't admit it.

"Well, she's probably faking it. Put her on the couch and see if she responds when I pull out my sword!" He whirled around, yanked his sword from its sheath around his waist and swished it in the air near her head. He hoped his quick movement and threat would frighten her enough into jumping and showing everyone she was really okay, but she didn't move.

"Ethan, this is a travesty. I need her!" Garcia thought of no one but himself as he finally tried to see if there was some way to revive his treasure hunter. Ethan's look of astonishment took Garcia off guard. Ethan thought to himself, *Does he seriously not see that this girl is about to die?*

Then, he spoke. "Captain, may I suggest we take a dingy to the shore line? I'll tie her so she can't escape then we'll let her in the water so she can heal."

"I don't know." Garcia's thoughts drifted.

Ethan couldn't believe it. Surely he must see this girl needs help! Ethan lay the girl on the couch as Garcia had previously suggested. Then, he turned around in his own act of defiance and faced Garcia. "You have three choices. Number one, you can let her die. If that happens, you will have a swarm of mermaids that take over the ship and kill you. No one else. Just you." Garcia looked at him.

"Number two, you can throw her back in and let her go. If this happens, you will have a swarm of mermaids that take over the ship and kill you. No one else. Just you." Garcia winced this time.

"Number three, you can do as I suggested and allow her to heal. Then she can find your treasure for you. Then you can take her back to Spain or whatever. But if the mermaids know she is still alive, they will let you live. For now." He paused. "They have so far."

Garcia knew he was right. "Fine. Take her to the water." But he added, "If she escapes, I will kill you." He had to maintain some sense of authority.

Chapter Twenty-Eight:
They're All on Their Way

The ship anchored just off the shore of a small island off the coast of Florida near Key West. This was a well-known shipping area and Garcia was concerned he may be spotted by a fisherman. Or worse, a Spanish Naval ship. Although he was flying the Spanish flag, Garcia's crew did not know he had been dishonorably discharged from the Navy. This attempt at finding the *Atocha* and her treasure was his only hope of getting back in the good graces of the king of Spain. If he was caught he would be executed for treason.

A small vessel with two shipmates and Ethan carrying Bew left the ship and made its way to the shore. Ethan feared the worst for Bew. They let the boat hit ground at the beach. It was sandy and would be easy to pull it up away from the waves. Ethan secured a rope around Bew's waist and walked into the waves with her. He feared what other mermaids would do if they saw him so he didn't secure the other end of the rope to himself. He allowed her feet and the bottom of her body to drift in the water while he held on to the rest of her. He slowly began to lower more and more of her into the water. He began to see the color come back to her face and her hair began to flow in the water again. He knew she was healing. He began to breathe a sigh of relief.

Suddenly she began to struggle against him. Her arms and legs began to flail and her eyes were wide open. She yelled a horrible screeching yell. She was certainly all better now. Time to get back to the ship. He feared that her yell was a call for help and he couldn't risk a swarm of mermaids right now. Little did he know the call for help that she was really sending out. With her strength back, she was communicating like crazy.

Samuel and Elsie had stopped swimming long enough to meet each other along the way at a small underwater community of Swimmers who were friends of theirs. They supported Elsie's push for letting the Land

Runners know about the Swimmers. They'd followed Elsie's progress with Katharine and Madican's relationship with Emily to know that not all Land Runners were to be feared. Now Elsie and Samuel had to give them the bad news and ask for help. This community was not far off the coast from Key West.

Underwater communities are different in different regions. In the South where the water is warm there is abundant plant life. Much of the vegetation is used to create large homes and villages for the Swimmers, as wood or brick is used on Land Runners' homes. Inside the home of Aubrey and Christian, Samuel and Elsie began to tell them about Bew. Aubrey and Christian had been their friends forever.

A coral reef runs along the outskirts of the Florida Keys. It is enormous in size and full of life. There is coral, fish, dolphins, turtles and many others. It is a beautiful and desired place to live. The reef is also full of secret caves. Aubrey had found one the day that she and Christian had met so they decided to make it their home. They'd used the green seaweed for an overhang to the entrance of the cave. But under the seaweed, the sides were open. That was common in these waters too because the currents can be very strong during hurricanes and the homes underwater should be as prepared as the homes above water. Hanging from the seaweed ceiling were seashells and a few items from Elsie's visits to the shores of the Land Runners. The couple had offered Samuel and Elsie something to eat. Elsie suggested they try to nourish themselves before meeting up with the ship because they were going to need their strength. Samuel was about to try to eat when he heard Bew's voice.

"Heeeeeeeeellp!" She was close.

Samuel jumped up and began swimming. Because sonar telepathy doesn't work well when Swimmers are actually swimming, Elsie didn't know why Samuel was leaving so suddenly, but she knew him well enough to know that he must have a good reason. She gave Aubrey a knowing look and took off after Samuel. Aubrey and Christian decided they should follow. Christian slowed his swimming and began to call others in their community.

Elsie looked for Samuel because he was not answering her calls. She finally saw him hovering at the surface about fifty yards in front of her. She was by his side in seconds. She popped up out of the water and looked at him.

TIDELINES

"Sam, what is it?"

He answered her in his mind. "Turn around."

Elsie turned around and peered into the distance toward the shore. She could make out a large ship. But it wasn't just any ship. It was the ship she had seen approach the isle of Bryce that day. The one she tried to warn Pearl about. It was the ship that held her daughter.

"Let's go," she insisted.

"No. It isn't safe," Samuel answered. "I've been talking to Bew. She's okay now. They let her go in the water, and she's back to normal."

Elsie began to sob and protest. Samuel knew how much Elsie wanted to pursue that ship, right then. But he knew it was not the smart way to rescue Bew. Without the element of surprise, he could compromise the rescue. He needed to keep Elsie from trying to save Bew all by herself. It was hard to do because Elsie was so headstrong and stubborn, and she loved Bew so much. Aubrey and Christian arrived by their sides and saw Elsie crying. They also saw the ship in the distance and understood immediately that it was the ship holding Bew.

Samuel continued. "I've also talked to Madican. They're all on their way."

THEY'RE ALL ON THEIR WAY

Chapter Twenty-Nine: We'll Be There by Dusk

"Listen up!" Katharine didn't have to yell too loudly. Her shipmates were quick to stop and listen whenever she began to bark out orders. "Samuel and Elsie have found Bew!" The ship erupted in cries of relief and cheers. Madican put his arm around Emily and she began to cry. "She has been in the water and is better now, but still being held captive. She was abducted by Garcia as we suspected. The Swimmers are closing in, but they will still need our help to rescue her." She continued. "We will be there by dusk, so I suggest you get some sleep. Tomorrow you will need your strength."

Emily was so relieved to hear that Bew was alive. She had worried that the lack of consistent communication could mean the worst for Bew. But she knew Katharine wouldn't say Bew was okay if it weren't true.

"Madican, what are your parents saying? Where is she?" Emily was eager to learn more.

"She is on Captain Garcia's ship just like we thought." This time he was looking into her eyes just as he used to. "They want to use her to help locate the *Atocha* and the treasure. But Bew really doesn't know where it is. She's never been there. I've told her stories about it, but I'm not sure she would really be able to find it. Since Garcia thinks she does know where it is, she is playing along." Madican was taking it all in himself. He stopped for a minute, listening to his parents talk to him, then he continued.

"Bew says Ethan convinced Garcia to let him take her ashore so she could get in the water that would keep her alive. She feels good now, but knows to keep acting as if she is going to show them the location, until we can get to her. And she knows we're coming." Madican started to smile, thinking how he would be able to see his little sister again soon.

He was proud of her being so smart and helping them to rescue her. He looked at Emily and smiled even bigger. He leaned in and kissed her forehead. He was happy. He felt as if Bew's rescue was really coming now. And he had the girl of his dreams next to him.

Emily smiled when he kissed her forehead. She tried to remember if anyone had ever done that before, but she had no recollection. Not even her father had done that. She felt so comfortable with Madican now. It was as if they were one. He had always been able to finish her sentences, and he always knew what she was in the mood for to eat, but this closeness was different and special. They had an understanding. An understanding that they were meant to be together.

Chapter Thirty:
Time to Get Dressed

Elsie and Samuel stayed close to the ship and continued to talk with Bew and Madican most of the night. Aubrey and Christian helped locate more Swimmers willing to help rescue Bew. Right now, they didn't have a plan. But as soon as Katharine's ships arrived they would be able to determine the best course of action. Elsie knew Katharine would know what to do.

Emily had fallen asleep on Madican's shoulder late that night while they were sitting on the bench on the top level of the ship. As she began to wake she saw the sun rising on the horizon in the distance. Emily knew Katharine was steering them in the right direction. She felt that the sunrise was a sign. Now she wished she had brought her sketch book with her. The sunrise was one of the most beautiful she had ever seen and she felt the urge to capture it on paper. She imagined a picture of Madican asleep on the deck with the beautiful sunrise in the distance behind him. She closed her eyes and smiled at the thought. Her elbow nudged Madican to wake him. He stirred, then his eyes opened on Emily and he smiled. The two started to rise and stretch. They looked around and saw the crew hurrying around. This morning they were busy and seemed to be concentrating hard on completing their tasks. Emily saw Katharine at the edge of the ship peering through her spy glass. Emily squeezed Madican's hand as if to say "I'll catch up with you later." And began walking toward Katharine.

"What is it?" Emily asked cautiously.

Katharine stopped and looked down at Emily. "See for yourself." She handed her the spy glass.

Emily took the tool and began searching the water for whatever held Katharine's interest. She saw little black dots close to the horizon near the sun. Was this what Katharine was seeing? She looked up at Katharine with a questioning look.

Before she could speak Katharine said, "Look closer." Emily shifted the long tube so that objects further out were in focus. It was then that she saw them. Hundreds of Swimmers were heading toward them. They were jumping in and out of the water and making long, white bubbly streams in the water as they came closer. There were so many of them. Emily couldn't believe it. It made her shiver inside.

Katharine took the spyglass and said, "Come on I have something for you." Emily was full of questions but couldn't find the words. She obediently followed Katharine to her quarters.

Once inside, Emily sat down on the elaborate cot that Katharine used as a bed. It was more comfortable than she had imagined it would be. Katharine went toward her largest wooden chest, in the middle of the room. She took a key out of her pocket and opened it and lifted out a smooth red outfit. It closely resembled a uniform. It was slick looking with not a lot of ornamentation on it. The top was a jacket. It had gold and blue trimmed pockets with an appliqué design that she had not seen before. It was a fleur-de-lis, a symbol of strength used by many in France and in New Orleans. The bottom was a pair of long, sleek pants. The red color seemed to dance all over the fabric. Katharine walked toward Emily with the outfit. She passed through a family of sun rays that were slicing through the cracks in the walls and ceilings of Katharine's quarters. The sunlight shone on the outfit and Emily could make out shimmers in the fabric.

"This is for you." Katharine certainly didn't mix words.

Emily just stared at the extravagant outfit. She drew a blank and didn't know what to say. Katharine continued, "This was made for you by Elsie. I had hoped you would be traveling with me someday, and I wanted you to have something that would protect you."

Emily was still shocked. Katharine wasn't the only woman she knew who wore pants. Many of her female crew members wore pants. But Emily wasn't accustomed to them. She wasn't sure she could do it, but knew she had to. "It's beautiful," she finally squeezed a word out. She looked up and Katharine was smiling.

TIME TO GET DRESSED

"This is made mostly from seaweed and a few other items from the Swimmers' world. See how the fabric shines in the light? That's from the seashell fragments that were incorporated in the material for strength."

Emily suddenly looked up "For strength?" she asked, not sure why she would need a strong material.

"Well, you know what I do, Emily. And sometimes, actually more often than not, there is a lot of danger involved because I have to do a lot of fighting. Given what we're about to do for Bew, I thought this might come in handy for this trip." Katharine sat down next to Emily. "I know you're frightened. But I also know how strong you are in here." She said pointing to Emily's forehead. "This outfit is made of high-grade materials that can withstand the teeth of giant sharks so I believe it will serve you well against a sword." Katharine saw the look on Emily's eyes and realized she had just frightened her.

"I don't know if I can fight, Katharine!" Emily insisted. "I've never wielded a sword!" Katharine put her hand on Emily's knee as she saw it was shaking.

"Emily, the time may come when Bew may need your help, when we all need your help. We're all here to rescue her and we just don't know what we're going to encounter. You need to be prepared. This dress..."

Emily cut her off. "I know that it's scary for everyone, so I'm ready to do my part," she said with confidence. Emily had come to realize many things on that trip. She knew she was in love with Madican. She knew she had a strong bond with those close to her like Katharine and Brett and Pearl. But most importantly, she had found an inner strength in herself that she didn't know existed. She could control a small group, like the islanders back at Jesse's tavern, or command a large pirate ship. Just like this one.

She liked the feeling of her own strength. It scared her and excited her at the same time. She found that when she faced her fear of being in control and she overcame it, that the reward outweighed the fear. Katharine sat up straight and smiled at Emily's readiness. They both knew this was going to be a turning point in Emily's life. She had recently overcome some of her most haunting fears. It was the first time she had been on a ship since her family drowned, and she had come to realize that she was in love with Madican, and that he loved her too.

But Katharine knew Emily had to face her last fear—being in control of herself and others. Since Emily had come to live on the island, everyone had taken care of her. She never had an opportunity to take care of herself. Pearl was always telling her what to do, Brett was in charge of helping everyone else on the island. Katharine took care of the supplies and all the needs of the island. Besides her sketches, Emily had nothing to take care of.

Katharine knew that one day soon she would want to settle down, maybe with Jean, and leave the way of the pirate. When that happened, she would need a strong leader on the Isle of Bryce. Someone to control things when pirates and foreign ships came. And she knew Emily shouldn't depend on others all her life. She needed to learn to depend on herself. Emily needed to face her fear of taking care of herself and learn to take charge. Katharine had seen the spark in her when she took control of things back on the island when everyone was bustling around trying to form a plan. Emily had stepped up and took control by pointing everyone in the right direction.

"Emily, you have many natural instincts when it comes to fighting. Stand tall, never take your eye off your opponent and always be ready to defend yourself. They never expect a girl to be able to defend herself." Katharine pushed out a slight smile.

"I'll do my best," Emily said.

"This blouse and trousers will help protect you." Katharine continued to explain about the gift. "It's strong to keep the sharp points out, lightweight to keep you from getting too tired, and slick to help you swim if you need it." Katharine trailed off a bit on the last description.

"Swim?" Emily gulped.

"We normally fight in the ships on the water, Emily. There is always that chance. But remember what Pearl told you? Stay close to Madican. He won't leave your side. If you happen to go in the water, he'll be right there." She tried to sound convincing. But Katharine knew that in the heat of battle, should it come to that, that things can get confusing and crazy. She could lose Madican or he could lose her and if she did go overboard, well, Katharine just hoped the Swimmers would be ready. Emily nodded, understanding what Katharine was trying to tell her, and trying to convince herself everything would be all right. It had to be. For Bew. They both sat silent for a minute, understanding what this meant to everyone.

Then Emily stood up. "I guess I need to get dressed."

TIME TO GET DRESSED

Emily and Katharine emerged from Katharine's cabin. All eyes turned and stared at Emily's new appearance. Madican met her eyes and smiled deeply at her as if to say *You look perfect*. Katharine led Emily to the middle of the ship and announced that Emily would be taking control of the ship. The crew cheered at their new leader. Unknown to Emily, Katharine had already discussed the decision with her first four shipmates in command, Milo, Anna, Morgan and Jacob. She would allow all control to go to Emily, with her supervision for now, and they were to adhere to Emily's commands. Katharine would be in the background but they would be following Emily's lead.

Emily asked for the spyglass and began to search for the Swimmers. They were much closer now and she tried to contact them with her thoughts. She learned that Elsie and Samuel's friends had reached out to all the Swimmers near the islands in the Caribbean. All had agreed to come help. Most knew Samuel and Elsie and were glad to help them in any way. Emily knew it was time to make some decisions and form a plan of action.

Chapter Thirty-One: She's Not Going to Be Helping Us Today

Bew blinked her eyes. She had tried to sleep but the ship was not a comfortable place for a little girl. The trip had been rough on her. She was weak and scared. But she knew her family was close. The dark room filtered in little light. To move her arms and legs was still difficult because she had been without water for so long. Her limbs were sore and her muscles cramped a lot since Ethan had let her go in the water. All she knew was that she wanted to be back with her family. She tried to stretch and move her legs when she felt the shackle on her ankle. It was tight and pushed into her skin. Swimmers' skin is different from Land Runners' skin and the shackle felt like it was cutting into her when she tried to move.

If she had a mirror she would see the dirt on her face and body. They'd kept her in little boys' clothes that were too baggy. They were damp from being in the cold wet cabin of the ship, and had collected what looked like every piece of dust from the rest of the ship. Her pants were held up with a rope. The other end of which was tied to a large metal handle on the wall of the cabin. She tried to make out any images in the room but her eyes were also weak. She listened for noises outside the cabin and heard many men shuffling around. Their footsteps were quick and solid. She assumed they were hurrying to find the location of the three small islands that formed a triangle off the coast of Florida, which was the description of the location of the sunken *Atocha* that she had made up to fool her captors. She had no idea where the sunken ship was. That was Madican who would go there and explore the ocean depths. Bew had no desire to see such a thing. But she played along as if she knew where it was so the strange man they called Captain Garcia wouldn't kill her. She began to hear a steady set of footsteps coming closer to her cabin. She closed her eyes and pretended to be asleep.

The door to the cabin was pushed open and Captain Garcia entered along with two other men. The two men had on a strange clinging outfit. It was black and shiny. They looked strange to her. The captain approached her. When he saw she was asleep he tapped her with his foot to wake her.

"Get up," he insisted. She opened her eyes and attempted to sit up. The shackle and the rope were painful. He saw how she grimaced as she moved but this didn't seem to affect him. He knew he had to find that treasure fast. By now, the rest of the mermaids would be headed toward him and he assumed he had little time. He knelt down next to her and spoke through his teeth. "Today you will show me where the three islands can be found. And today you will take these two divers to the shipwreck." He motioned to the two men in the shiny black material standing behind him. "Do I need to tell you what will happen to you if you don't?" Bew raised her eyes to meet his and she shook her head slowly. She was a strong defiant little girl. This man scared her but she wasn't going to let him see her fear.

"Good." He stood up. "Now get up and come to the bow of the ship with me." One of the shiny black-dressed men came over and untied her rope while Garcia took a chain from around his neck. The chain held a key that unlocked the shackle. Once lose, Bew rubbed her ankle. It was red and swollen from the pain. She tried to move her foot back and forth but it was too stiff. The shiny black dressed man held her by her arm and assisted her while she stood. Together they all walked out onto the main deck of the ship. Bew immediately shielded her eyes from the bright light of the sun. Although the sunlight hurt, she was glad to see it because that meant the Swimmers would be able to see better. And find her better. She had talked to her mom, Elsie, that morning and she knew they were close. Elsie had told her that hundreds of Swimmers were coming and Katharine and her two ships, and Longskull and his two ships, and even Emily and Brett. She was filled with gratitude to know that they were all coming to help her. Elsie told her to keep playing along and making them think she knew where the treasure was. She said she would tell her when they were coming and it would be very soon. Probably that day.

Garcia took the rope from the shiny black-dressed man and led Bew to a large table in the middle of the deck. On it was an old, round map, a compass, and two spyglasses. Bew wished only for a bowl of water.

"Now, girl, this is a map of this area. We are two miles off the coast of the southernmost tip of the region known as Florida. According to this map there are no islands that form a triangle anywhere." He paused for effect and stared at Bew. She didn't flinch so he continued. "I certainly don't think you would lie to me. Would you?" He almost looked like he was pouting. Bew shook her head. "Okay, so why don't you point to the triangle islands on this map, because I just don't see it." Bew looked at the map and knew she had to think of something fast.

"Maybe this map is too old," she stuttered.

Without warning Garcia raised his arm up and knocked Bew to the floor. Bew lay there. She was in a great deal of pain. The vision of the ship's railing began to blur in her eyes. She tried to focus on a seagull flying in the distance but it too became blurry and eventually disappeared. The shapes around her were fuzzy and the colors were melting together until everything was dark.

Garcia kicked Bew's unconscious body and realized she wasn't going to be of any help to him that day.

"Ethan!" Garcia bellowed for his first mate. He looked around and realized several of the crew members were standing around watching him. They'd stopped their duties when they heard the smack from Garcia's backhand hitting Bew's face. They stood motionless with mouths open, shocked that he had hit the little girl. They were sure that was not a permitted action by the government of Spain. Ethan was pushing his way through the crowd toward Garcia when he saw Bew lying on the floor of the ship.

"What's happening?" Ethan's tone was stern but he was careful not to be disrespectful to his captain.

"She's not going to be helping us today, Ethan. I want you to take her back to the galley and lock her up."

Ethan obeyed and lifted Bew up to carry her down the ship. Silently he questioned the actions of his superior. He knew finding the treasure was important, but he didn't agree with the harsh methods Garcia was using.

As Ethan carried Bew toward her confines, the crew stepped aside making room for them to pass. They hung their heads in respect as if the

SHE'S NOT GOING TO BE HELPING US TODAY

little girl was dead. Ethan wondered if some of the crew questioned their captain's harsh treatment of the girl. They were soldiers after all and soldiers didn't hit defenseless little girls. Even if the little girl was a mermaid. They did not like the way this mission was headed. After Ethan made his way through them they all turned their attention again toward Garcia.

"Okay, okay" Garcia yelled. "Nothing to see." His words were sarcastic. "Get back to work!"

Chapter Thirty-Two: A Big Family

In the main room of *The Black Susan*, Emily was meeting with Katharine, Brett, Elsie, Samuel, Longskull, and two of his mates. The room was about ten by thirteen and expertly decorated for Katharine to host guests while she was on the water or docked at some far-away secret cove. The floorboards were covered in Persian rugs and a silver chandelier hung from the ceiling beams. Matching sconces flanked the door and the window in the room. Dark wood benches sat along all the walls with silk throw pillows, like the ones in Katharine's chambers. In the middle of the room was a round wooden-base table with an elaborate pink and grey marble top. Several ornate boxes and glass containers of rum were spread out on the table, and some on the benches. Emily wondered what could be in the boxes while she led the discussion.

"We know where Garcia's ship is. Our best chance at a successful rescue will be to surprise him as much as possible. The Swimmers will come in from below. Their job will be to disassemble the rudder under the boat. That will prevent Garcia's crew from being able to control his ship. That's the easy part." She paused and scanned her small crowd of listeners to make sure they seemed to be following her directions so far. Then she continued. "We will take two of our ships into the cove where Garcia is and flank each side leaving him a clear exit out of the cove. He'll be scared and will attempt to leave the cove. He will raise his anchor and then find that he cannot control his ship. He will basically be drifting toward the shore, except the Swimmers will begin controlling the ship and will hold it steady for us."

The others nodded. The plan was starting. Elsie and Samuel were anxious. Their concern was for Bew's safety. But they needed to make sure that the Swimmer's identity remained a secret. "How do we know he'll be scared and try to run?" Elsie asked. "And how can we be sure he won't try to hurt Bew?"

"That's a good question, Elsie," Brett answered. "I think I can explain it. We know that Garcia is an arrogant man. He wants to think he is better than any pirate on these waters. He wants to think he is a better class of person, and a better soldier, or fighter, than any of us. But, the truth is he is very unsure of himself. Deep down he knows he can't fight us. His only hope will be to try to outrun us, taking Bew with him, and continue to search for the *Atocha*." Brett paused. "I strongly believe he won't hurt her because he needs her."

Emily continued. "The Swimmers will be below the belly of the ship controlling its direction. They won't let it move. When he finds he can't control his ship he will start to panic and that's when we will overtake it." Emily had to stop herself for a brief second. The thought of actually climbing aboard another ship scared her. But her confidence in herself was growing and she needed to remind herself that the mission was to save Bew. She couldn't be scared. She just had to do it.

Katharine saw Emily's slight hesitation and took over the discussion. "Once onboard our first and only goal will be to find Bew. She is communicating with us so that shouldn't be too hard. Once we have her, we're leaving immediately. We are not robbing this ship and we are not throwing anyone overboard. We simply get her to the water and get out of there. Once we're all back on *The Black Susan* and our other ships, all the Swimmers will leave the area. Including Elsie and her family, taking Bew and Madican with them." They all took a breath at hearing this. But they all knew it was for the best. They needed to get all the Swimmers away from there immediately. "Garcia's ship will be disassembled and it will eventually drift ashore, beaching itself in that cove."

Emily looked at Madican. She knew he had to go be with his family. She knew he needed to leave the area for his own safety. But it pained her to think of being away from him. Especially because she would be on the ship by herself. But for the first time that thought was not as scary as it used to be. She was beginning to feel more at ease on the water. She needed Madican's love, but for the first time, she was not sure she needed his protection as desperately as thought.

Samuel spoke up. "Katharine, what about the Isle of Bryce? Eventually Garcia will come looking for another Swimmer and he knows he can find us there." Elsie and Katharine exchanged stares. The two best friends had already discussed that and their conclusion was a sad one. The Swimmers would not be coming back to the island home they had been a part of for so long.

Emily saw their exchange and immediately knew what they were thinking. "No." she whispered. Her eyes began to fill with tears. This meant she would not see Madican or Bew again. She lowered her head and sobbed into her chest.

Madican came to her side and put his arm around her. He spoke to her thoughts to try to soothe her. "Em, I'll never really leave you. We may have to separate for a while until I know all the Swimmers have gone deep and everyone is safe. But I will come back for you. We are meant to be together. I am meant to be with you. My life is not a life without you." He was almost begging her not to cry. She looked up at him. His eyes were dull but he tried to smile at her anyway. She leaned up and kissed him gently and quickly. Then, she threw both arms around his neck and cried. They held on tight for a minute before Katharine spoke again.

"The Swimmers won't be safe on our island anymore. We're confident that Garcia will be too ashamed to make another attempt. We think he'll probably lose his title with the Spanish Government and he won't even have a boat. But we don't know who he has confided in. We can assume many of his crew know, but we don't know how much they have in the form of resources to attempt to capture another Swimmer. But it isn't a risk we can take. Elsie and I knew that our friendship, this island home that we all know, may someday be compromised and sadly today is that day. We Land Runners will return to the island and our way of life, but the Swimmers will move on." Katharine's voice quivered. She was shaken up at the thought of never seeing her friends again. Unable to stand it, she walked out of the room.

Emily's turn as the leader was now. Katharine was emotionally upset and Emily knew she needed to step up. "All right, we will be in position in the morning. As soon as the sun shows over the horizon we will engage our plan. Is everyone ready?" Emily looked over the small group. She thought she saw Longskull wipe away a tear. They all nodded and a few even answered with "Yes, ma'am."

Longskull and his two men made their way back to their ships to spread the message about the mission first thing in the morning. Elsie and Samuel headed to Katharine's chambers for an evening meal. Emily was left with Madican and Brett. They all sat in silence for a few minutes. Brett sensed the two needed to just be quiet for a minute. But he also knew he didn't want to just stand up and walk away from them yet. Brett had already been thinking about the future of the two. Madican and Emily were sitting together on one of the benches across the room from Brett. He rose and went to them, taking a seat next to them on an adjacent bench.

"I know these are tough times for our island family and for your family, Madican." He nodded at both Emily and Madican. Without using the word "love" he continued, "But, I think there may be a way for you to be able to continue your relationship." The two listened intently as Brett discussed their future with them for hours.

Dawn came early as Emily found herself not being able to sleep. She was anxious and excited at the same time. These emotions were new to her and she didn't know how to sort them out. She knew they had to save Bew first, but after that what would she do when Madican had to go into hiding? Would she just go back to life on the Isle of Bryce? Would Katharine officially hand over control of *The Black Susan* to Emily? If that happened she'd have to pursue a life of a pirate. Which wasn't so bad, but she didn't want any kind of life without Madican. It all went back to him. All her thoughts were leading to him. She contemplated what Brett had suggested the night before, but wasn't able to put all the pieces together just yet. She needed to concentrate on the rescue today.

Overwhelmed at the idea of a future without Madican, she finally got up and hoped a little fresh air would help clear her mind. They would be fighting to get Bew back that day and she needed a clear head. She stepped out onto the main deck. The crew members were already shuffling around. The main sail was not up yet because it wouldn't hang until she gave the order. When the crew saw her emerge they stopped. Pirate crews don't salute. Most of the time, a pirate is too busy to stop and salute or to stand at attention. But they acknowledge their captain by slightly nodding in his or her direction, to let the captain know the crew member is paying attention to their orders. Emily knew that a slight wave of her hand told them that she was grateful they were paying attention. This interaction was something she had seen Katharine do, so she assumed it was the proper protocol for a new pirate captain.

Emily approached the side of the ship and surveyed the horizon. To her right was land about three miles away. To her left was the great green ocean, dotted with Swimmers diving in and out. She felt confident with their help. The idea of having to attack Garcia's ship without their help was unthinkable. Their loyalty to one of their own was admirable. She felt that loyalty toward her own island family—Pearl and Brett and the others. She would do anything for them. Her newfound confidence felt good as she thought about fighting off anyone who would try to hurt her family. That's what it was. She smiled to herself. *A big family.*

Katharine walked over and stood with Emily. She didn't say anything but she put her hand on Emily's shoulder.

Emily looked at her and said, "It's time, isn't it?"

"Yes."

Chapter Thirty-Three:
MAN YOUR STATIONS!

During this trip, Emily had found a new comfort at being on the water. She had always loved to watch the waves and the crest of the horizon where the ocean kisses the sky. She and Madican would spent time on the tidelines and would both stare at the horizon together. It was their time to be together without anyone else around. Their time for their friendship, their relationship, to flourish. It wasn't the Land Runners' home or the Swimmers' home. It was just their space. But now she felt more drawn to his home. He called it the land under the water. She used to laugh at his description, trying to seem as if she understood what land under water was. After this journey she felt she belonged on the water. Or in it. She knew taking on this new role of pirate captain was invigorating. And she liked it. She hoped that when they were able to rescue Bew that she and Madican would somehow be able to continue a life together.

She was at the helm when Madican stepped up to join her.

"Emily, you look like you have everything under control," he assured her.

She looked at his warm eyes and felt comfort in his words and his smile. He stared at her with that smile like no one else could. His confidence was giving her strength. She had let her hair down that day and braided it behind her. The long lock was tucked into the back of the red blouse so it wouldn't be in the way. But she suddenly had the urge to pull it out and let it hang on her back and neck. She reached up and untucked it, letting it fall behind her. Madican smiled at this feminine gesture. He was glad to see a bit of her soft side since she had been trying so hard to be so confident and in control lately.

"We're a little over an hour away, Madican. Are you ready?" she asked with the voice of a captain.

"Yes, ma'am." He saluted her and then bowed.

"Oh, don't be silly." She giggled. "I want to make sure everyone is ready." Her voice became flat again.

Madican took the hint and responded by putting his hands on her shoulders "We're all ready. Just call the commands like Katharine does. Stay in communication with me. I will be talking to other Swimmers on Longskull's two boats and they will direct him as to what you say. He is ready to follow your lead." Emily nodded and smiled. She was ready. Ready to get this over with.

Before a pirate attacks another ship, there is a period of quiet to reflect on the task at hand and to prepare mentally for an impending fight. Emily's crew were silent. They went about their normal tasks for preparing the ship and themselves, but no one spoke a word. They were not far from the cove and they would be waiting for Emily's direction. But for now, they reflected in silence. This gave Emily the chance to reflect too. She watched the waves and the dolphins and Swimmers jump. They seemed to be dancing on top of the water. In the distance, Longskull's two ships were flanking her, waving their long, skinny flags. Katharine and Emily were standing together, in silence watching the dance.

"They do this before a battle," Katharine whispered.

Emily was slightly shocked that Katharine had spoken. "What do you mean by battle? Swimmers battle?" Emily whispered back.

"Oh, yes," Katharine said. "Land Runners and Swimmers both battle within themselves. Over land or money or love." Emily still looked perplexed. She never thought about Swimmers actually fighting. But if Land Runners could do it, then she figured Swimmers could too.

Katharine continued. "The Swimmers have a very intricate swim that they do before a battle to help prepare them. It consists of jumps and dives out of the water and twists and turns before diving back in. The really good ones can do jumps and dives as partners. It's beautiful to watch."

"You've seen this before?" Emily was intrigued.

"Yes. Many times. Elsie and Samuel are not the normal ones to fight, but I've been around for a few of them. Elsie loves to participate in the dance too. She and Samuel are beautiful together."

Emily smiled at the thought of this whole new world that she didn't know existed out there. So much of Madican's world was unknown to her. Her desire to learn more about it and to become a part of it, like

MAN YOUR STATIONS!

Katharine was, gave her strong hope that she and Madican would be together.

The entrance to the cove was on the horizon now. Emily closed her eyes and spoke to Madican. "Where are you?"

"I'm swimming right next to your ship."

"We're about there. Has Elsie been talking to Bew?"

"Yes, she knows to be ready. She knows we're coming. She is weak again, but I know as soon as we get there and we can get her in the water her strength will come back."

"Good. Is everyone ready?"

"Yes."

"*The Black Susan* will go in first along with the *Billie Jean*. Longskull's ships will stay just outside the cove."

There was silence while Madican relayed the command to his counterpart on Longskull's ship. Emily took this opportunity to open her eyes. As soon as she did a strong gust pushed over the ship and whipped the main sail, the canvas making a loud crack. Emily shook, but not as much as she had the first time she'd heard that sound on the ship. She raised her head, stuck out her chest, and straightened her back. She was in charge now. And it was time to get Bew.

"Man your stations!" she bellowed. Her command was echoed by lesser crew men throughout the ship as her instructions were shared with everyone on board. She began to walk the deck with speed and urgency. She stopped once to look through the spyglass to see the opening of the cove getting closer. As the ship proceeded toward the break, Emily began to make out the tip of a ship's sail. Slowly the flag came into view. It was them! The flag bore the Spanish mark of its Navy. They had found the ship. As *The Black Susan, Billie Jean* and Longskull's second ship became increasingly visible to the Spanish ship, a large horn sounded from Garcia's crew. They had seen Emily approaching and were sending a warning signal that they were a government vessel, not to be interfered with.

"Madican, send the Swimmers in now. We've been seen," Emily instructed.

Silence.

"Emily, slow your pace. The Swimmers are not close enough yet. Give them time to get into the cove before you," Madican finally instructed.

"Got it."

Emily turned to her lead crewman. "Lower the sails to slow our pace. We want them to think we might be reconsidering coming in after them. That will give the Swimmers time to get in there to disassemble the rudder without being noticed." Immediately the crewman went to work yelling orders at everyone. Emily spoke to Madican, who instructed the other three boats.

MAN YOUR STATIONS!

Chapter Thirty-Four: Seaweed and Seashells

Garcia had been informed that two pirate ships were approaching and had ordered the anchors be raised in case a swift escape were necessary.

"Sir, we think they may have seen the Spanish Flag and are reconsidering an attack. The reputation of the Spanish Navy proceeds it, even among the pirate's culture." This made Garcia smile. He was no longer a member of the Navy but was able to use its reputation to support his task.

"Good. They should think twice. But just to be sure tell the crew to man their canons and be ready."

"Yes, sir."

"And bring me Ethan." Garcia paced while he waited for his confidante to join him. He knew this pirate boat was no coincidence, there just weren't that many of them anymore. The girl mermaid was why they were here. He knew it. But mermaids and pirates? That was new. He hadn't expected that.

Soon Ethan rushed in. "You asked for me?"

"Yes. It's about the girl. You no doubt know that there are pirate ships approaching." Garcia turned away from Ethan.

"Yes, sir."

"Well, why do you think that is?" His tone was derisive.

"The girl?" This was more of a statement from Ethan because he already had a pretty good idea.

"Exactly," Garcia said with a whip of his finger through the air.

"But sir, they are pirates, not mermaids." Ethan decided to act as if he didn't know anything at all and that Garcia was the only one who could possibly figure it out.

"Don't you know anything? Mermaids and pirates go hand in hand. They support each other." Garcia began moving around the cabin in circles. "The mermaids depend on the pirates to supply them with food and goods. And the pirates use the mermaids to find the treasures of the sea. Gold and jewels mean nothing to mermaids. They just like seaweed and seashells." Garcia liked to pretend to know everything.

"Wow, sir, for someone who has been so involved with the Spanish Navy for so many years, I'm amazed that you found time to learn so much about mermaids." Ethan could be sarcastic without anyone knowing it.

"Ethan, we must hide the girl. If they don't turn around we can be assured they will want to come aboard."

"But, sir, I know you have thought about our ability to stop them in their tracks right now by just using our cannons, right?"

Garcia stood straight. "Yes. The crew should be manning them now."

Just then, a young crewman burst into the cabin. "Sir, we are drifting! The shipmates can't control the movement of the ship."

Chapter Thirty-Five:
Bew's Curse

"Emily, the ship's rudder is detached. Garcia can't control his ship." Madican's news was exciting to hear. *The Black Susan* and *Billie Jean* were slowly making their way into the cove and positioning themselves to flank either side of Garcia's ship.

"Raise the sail!" Emily yelled. "Proceed ahead full!" She looked over to Katharine, who was watching Emily's moves. Emily raised her spyglass and surveyed the length of Garcia's ship. She felt the wind pick up and her ship begin to feel as if it was moving faster. She gave the same instructions to Madican. Her adrenaline was pumping and she was filled with energy. She watched as *Billie Jean* began to sail a bit faster too. She was ready to move now. She was ready to fight for Bew.

As her ship got closer, she saw Bew on the deck being held by Ethan. The sight of him took her by surprise. She had hoped that he didn't have anything to do with the girl's kidnapping. She had hoped he was different. But he held Bew tight, and she was tied around the waist to her hands and her mouth was gagged.

"Em-uh-leeeeee!" She heard Bew scream out to her and it almost made her sick to her stomach with grief. *Oh, Bew!* That sweet voice she had not heard in such a long time. "We're here, Bew!" she called back.

"Help me, Em!"

Emily paced as she struggled to not feel helpless. She could see Bew and talk to her in her mind, but she could not reach out and grab her. A huge river of water stood between her ship and Garcia's ship. She felt helpless, and hated that feeling.

"Emily, hurry!" Bew yelled.

She took a deep breath, shook off any remaining fear, then barked the order, "Bring me a horn!" Immediately someone rushed up and handed her a sounding horn. Emily put it to her mouth and pointed it in the direction of Garcia, who was standing on the edge of his ship laughing at the young female pirate.

"Garcia! We just want the girl!" Emily yelled at him.

She could see him look down and around and then start laughing. Was he laughing at her? Did he not think she was serious? *Really?*

"Give me the girl or your ship and all on it will sink." Her voice was steady and loud.

Garcia took an opportunity to attempt to have a little fun at Emily's expense, "Oh, but then you'll be killing the girl, too."

Emily wasn't playing. And she certainly wasn't letting someone not take her seriously. "We both know she will swim. And we both know what will happen to you and your crew underwater with all her family waiting for you." She emphasized the word family, yet was amazed at how heartless she could sound. She noticed Garcia peering over the side of the ship looking into the water. The Swimmers were deep so he couldn't see anyone. They intentionally wanted to appear at first as if there was no one there at all.

He began to laugh. "You're bluffing! My boat has ten cannons. I don't see but four on yours. You are outgunned. Now move your ships so mine may pass."

"How can you pass if you can't control your ship? Look at the hill on the left bank. Find a point of reference and you will see your ship is drifting closer to the shore. Your rudder is disassembled. You cannot control your ship. If you fire upon me, I will fire back. You may destroy my ship but yours will be damaged and will sink too. And then you will meet her family. Don't believe me? Look into the water again."

"*Now*, Mad!" Emily told Madican to have all the Swimmers surface. When Garcia peered over the side of his ship this time he was shocked at the number of mermaids he saw. It looked like thousands to him, all hovering on the surface of the water. Some jumped out and dove back. This was an intimidation trick among Swimmers. Garcia saw a glass landscape dotted with hundreds of heads, all ready to rescue the girl he was holding prisoner. The image was powerful. The mermaids moved and jumped. They swam around the ship and in one movement began approaching his ship. Emily watched Garcia stare in horror as the dots slowly made their way in unison toward him. Then silently, without a splash or a droplet, they all sunk deep out of sight. But they were not out of his mind. He knew they were there, silently lurking in the dark water below. And he knew he could no longer control his ship. But he was not going down without a fight.

"Well, you certainly have my attention," he said. His crew was shocked by his statements. They were ready to surrender after seeing the army of mermaids coming toward them, so they couldn't imagine why he was toying with her.

"Garcia, what are you *doing*?" Ethan asked.

"Shut up!" Garcia yelled back. "I'm going to convince that young pirate in red to come over here, then I'll release the mermaid and hold the pirate for ransom instead." The fire in his eyes was roaring. Ethan wasn't so sure that Garcia was still thinking clearly.

Emily answered Garcia. "Good, now release the girl into the water."

"You'll need to come and get her. She isn't feeling up to swimming." Garcia beckoned.

Brett stood next to Emily. "Don't go, Emily. You can tell he's planning a trap."

Emily was scared. Her fear was doing its best to overcome her again. She didn't want to go over there. He just needed to put Bew in the water and let them all go on their merry ways. She didn't want the confrontation. "How should I answer him?"

"Tell him you'll come. Then we'll disguise Katharine as you and send her along with many others. She can fight him." Brett tried to convince Emily. But the thought of someone else fighting her battles was not okay. This was her fight and she was not going to go running to Katharine.

"No, here's what we'll do. I'm going over there. Katharine said my new suit is very strong so I'll be fine. I don't intend on fighting anyone. I'll just make a straight line to Bew. Get Ethan away from her fast enough to get her overboard."

"I know you want to be in control of this, but sending you just isn't safe." Katharine tried to interject.

"None of this is safe," Emily said. "If you want to come with me, fine, but I'm going. Bring us in closer!" she yelled before Katharine could protest. The crew looked to Katharine as if to receive her approval before following this new young pirate's orders. Katharine looked at the ground but nodded so the crew would proceed. She had handed over *The Black Susan* to Emily and it was now hers to command.

Emily stood at the edge of the ship and yelled to Garcia, "I'm coming! Lower your planks!"

When the ships were close, ropes were thrown back and forth to ensure Garcia's ship wouldn't drift away toward the shore and take *The Black Susan* with it. Long planks were balanced between the ships to let crew go back and forth. Emily led the invasion with Katharine and Brett close at her heels. Katharine was determined not to let anything happen to Emily. When the crew jumped onto the deck, Emily saw Ethan carry Bew toward the back of the ship and into a cabin with no apparent windows. The team was met with soldiers bearing swords and it wasn't long before the blades were flashing. Emily was running toward the cabin while Brett, Katharine, and the others were fighting off the soldiers.

"Hold on Bew, I'm coming!" Emily tried to talk to her but with all the commotion it was hard to get a message through. The crew from *Billie Jean* had boarded the ship too and were also met with sword-wielding soldiers. Emily found herself with soldiers on either side of her. She really had no experience fighting so she pulled out her sword and started swinging it around like a mad woman, just making large round circles and screaming. The soldiers backed away and looked for other pirates to fight. She kept making her way toward the dark cabin, looking for Garcia along the way. But there was no sign of him anywhere.

There were plenty of pirates to help fight the soldiers. Some of the soldiers actually decided to take their chances with the mermaids and jumped overboard rather than fight a pirate. It was looking like the soldiers were outnumbered. But Emily didn't see Garcia, and she had to get to the cabin. She looked around and saw Katharine and Brett and the others, actually telling the soldiers to jump rather than killing them. She loved that about Katharine.

"Em-uh-leeee! Help!" she heard Bew scream for her.

"Where are you?" Emily called.

Silence.

"Madican! Where are you?" Emily wanted to know if he was talking to Bew.

Silence.

Emily saw a clear path to the cabin and ran toward it, running harder than she did on their island. When she got to the door she yanked on it and was surprised to find it open. Her surprise caused her to pause for a second. A brief second, but just long enough for two huge arms to grab her, pull her inside the cabin, and throw her to the floor. The darkness was maddening but somehow, she knew Bew was in there too.

"You stupid girl!" Garcia yelled at her and kicked her hard in the gut.

Emily let out a cough and moan. The kick had stunned her but amazingly she was not in that much pain. Her suit had worked. She figured she should pretend to be more hurt than she actually was.

"Ethan, tie her up," Garcia barked.

Emily felt him kneel over her and tie her hands behind her back. When she was grabbed, her sword must have fallen on the floor somewhere. It wouldn't be any good to her now with her hands tied. Ethan leaned over her and whispered, "Shhhh." *What was that supposed to mean?* she thought. Then she realized he had not tied her hands quite as tightly as she would have. She tried to adjust her eyes to the lack of light and slowly made out Bew's figure in the corner. "Bew!"

"Emily, I'm so scared." Bew told her in her mind.

"Everyone is here now. We're going to take over the ship soon and get you off here. The Swimmers are surrounding the ship. If you see a chance to jump off, do it! They'll be there to get you and untie you."

"My ankles hurt. I'm not sure I can walk."

"It's okay. Madican and others will be here soon. He'll get you back in the water."

Just then Brett broke through the door. He held his hand up to try to see in the darkness. That was the move Garcia needed. He kicked him in the gut knocking him down and blocking the door. Brett screamed at the pain. Emily yelled, "Brett!"

"Emily?!"

"Bew and I are here!"

Emily looked out the door and saw Katharine holding her own with the soldiers. Garcia grabbed Emily and Ethan gathered up Bew, and together they made their way out the back door to the cabin with the two girls. They were met with Madican standing tall right outside the door. Garcia and Ethan stopped in their tracks. Emily's heart fluttered when she realized he was there to save her. Her and Bew.

Garcia held Emily tight and yelled at Madican, "Get out of our way! If you try to stop me these girls both die!" Madican just smiled at him, taunting him to make a move. Madican loved Emily and loved his sister and no one was going to hurt either girl. He circled his sword in the air daring Garcia or Ethan to try something.

"I mean it, boy!" Garcia yelled. Emily was suddenly overcome with such a strong feeling of love for Madican that she became angry when Garcia called him a boy. She took the opportunity to stomp hard on his foot. Garcia doubled over and loosened his grip on her enough for her to pull away. He realized what she was doing and tightened his grip on her arm. "You're not going anywhere."

Emily looked at Madican and realized he had a decision to make—save her or save Bew. She knew what she had to do. She would not put him in that position. She looked Garcia in the face and said, "If you let her go, the Swimmers, I mean, uh, mermaids, will all go away too. Then, it will just be us against you. A fair fight."

Garcia was about to answer when Madican stopped him. "No, Emily. I can't let you do that."

Emily answered him silently, "I love you, Mad. You must take Bew and get out of here. Katharine and Brett will take care of me. I'll be fine. Just get her out of here!"

Garcia spoke up. "How do I know they will all leave?" Ah, she had hit a sore spot. He was scared of all the Swimmers. This was her best shot.

"You can stab me with my sword if they don't." She knew her suit would protect her, but Madican didn't.

"Don't be crazy, Emily!" he yelled out loud.

"I'm not being crazy. You take the Swimmers and the girl and get out of here and he won't stab me. Will you, Captain?" she turned toward Garcia. Emily silently told Madican about the suit, but he was not convinced and thought it was a horrible idea. He didn't want to leave her.

Garcia grabbed Emily and headed for the front of the cabin where the fighting was going on. He nodded to Ethan to follow along with Bew. Madican was behind Ethan, watching Bew closely for any opportunity to grab her and throw her over the side where his family was waiting. He was silently talking to her about this plan. She was very weak and would not survive a fall from the ship much longer.

"Attention!" Garcia held a knife to Emily's neck while Ethan cradled a tied-up Bew in his arms, with Madican on his heels.

Almost everyone stopped fighting when they heard this. Some shuffled to attention when they began to see others stop. Eventually all eyes were on Garcia and his prizes. Katharine was livid. Brett was still in pain but holding his own against two soldiers when they all stopped and stared at Garcia to listen to what he had to say.

"This young pirate here is your captain. She has agreed to stay on and fight me alone if I just agree to let this younger girl go." Splashing could be heard in the waters below.

"I think not." Garcia had changed his course. "I think I'll kill them both if you don't all leave my ship at once."

Ethan had been contemplating Garcia's actions this whole time. He knew the weak state the little girl was in. He began to see that Garcia's plan was only going to put him and the other crew members and soldiers in deep trouble with the mermaids, these pirates, and not to mention the King of Spain. He was not sure exactly what he would do.

Katharine slowly stepped forward. "I don't think you are going to kill either of these girls, Garcia."

Garcia tightened his grip on Emily as Katharine took another slow step forward. She was graceful when she fought, like she was when she did anything. Emily was impressed with her calmness and her confidence.

Ethan did not want to fight either of these female pirates. He wanted to go home and get away from there now. He didn't want to be drowned by a mermaid and he didn't want the King of Spain to hang him for screwing up this mission. He knew if he let this girl go he might be able to get out of there without the mermaids hurting him. But he wasn't sure Garcia would protect him from the King's wrath. But then again, it didn't look like Garcia was going to come out on the winning side of this battle. He realized his best interest was to let the girl go and help the pirates fight this crazy Garcia. He backed up slowly and loosened his grip on Bew. She felt his grip change and she could tell he was changing his allegiance. She silently told Madican that she thought he was about to let her go. Madican positioned himself in case that happened.

Katharine stopped just feet from Garcia. He sneered his old wrinkled face at her and spat in her direction, "You don't know what I am capable of."

Katharine noticed Ethan stepping back and slowly lowering Bew. Madican was inching closer to her. She looked so weak. Garcia had not noticed yet. Katharine knew she had to keep Garcia's attention. Suddenly everyone was talking in her head at once. She could tell that Emily could hear it too. Emily's eyes were blinking as if she was blinded as she was trying to make out what everyone was saying.

Madican was warning the Swimmers that he was about to jump over with Bew. There were Swimmers there to grab her quickly and untie her and get her out of the cove.

That meant Madican was about to leave her. Her heart sank as she realized this may be the last time she saw him. She wriggled in Garcia's arms and tried to turn to see him before he jumped. Garcia held tight and turned to see what she was trying to see. All he saw was Ethan standing empty handed with his arms down by his sides looking confused, and Madican standing on the railing of the ship. He held Bew tight and her bound hands were looped around her big brother's neck. She turned and looked at Garcia and gave him a stare that no pirate or bad Spaniard could ever imitate, a stare from her soul and her gut and the very bottom of the ocean. She swore to get revenge on him someday and cursed him in his mind, letting him hear her thoughts. He shuddered at her stare while he heard her words. Just then Madican and Bew let themselves fall off the side of the ship into the waters of the cove where their family waited.

Garcia snapped back to reality and whipped back around facing Katharine and Brett only a foot away from him. Brett grabbed at Emily but Garcia still had the knife on her neck. Katharine lunged at him while Emily pried at his arm. Suddenly Garcia stiffened and dropped the knife, a look of shock and confusion on his face. Emily pulled away from him as he fell to his knees. His thump on the wooden plank of the deck could be heard all over the cove in and out of the water. Behind him stood Ethan holding a blood-covered knife. Garcia fell face first on the deck. His body shook quickly then became still. They all looked around at each other, then at Ethan.

"I, I, uh, I just couldn't let him hurt you." Ethan said to Emily.

Emily rushed to Brett and he held her while she faced Ethan. "I can't believe any of this," Emily said. "You helped to kidnap that little girl and now you've killed Garcia." She stopped and looked at Katharine.

"Just what is your plan now, Ethan?" Katharine lowered her sword. Her former crew members, who now sailed for Emily, lowered their swords in unison. She knew her mission was over and this young man posed no threat any longer.

"I don't know."

Emily left the comfort of Brett's arms and ran to the tip of the ship that was facing the entrance to the cove. She saw both of Longskull's ships waiting to assist, and hundreds of Swimmers cresting the water while swimming away. That meant Bew was okay and they were leaving the cove. That also meant more communication was forbidden. She slowly closed her eyes and tried to talk to Madican.

"I know you can hear me. I want you to know that I will always love you. I am so happy Bew is okay. Please give her my love. Garcia is dead. I'll be heading back with Katharine now. I don't know what I'll do next, but please keep Brett's suggestion in your mind. I know I said I wasn't sure that was a good idea, but now I am so sure. I don't want a life without you. If you love me too, you'll meet me there." Emily stopped. She felt as if she had so much to say. Madican had left so fast they didn't have a chance to discuss their future. She knew the Swimmers would be gone from her life now forever and nothing made her feel worse than that.

Emily turned around and faced the crew of soldiers and pirates all still standing trying to decide what they were supposed to do next. Garcia was dead and many of his soldiers seemed to not be shaken by this. They all were looking toward Ethan for direction.

Elsie and Samuel had communicated to Katharine that they had Bew and Madican and were headed out of the cove. Katharine knew her friendship with Elsie would forever be forbidden by the counsel of Swimmers. Their relationship had endangered Bew and it was not something the Swimmers were ready to take a chance with again.

Emily watched as Ethan begged Katharine to let them go.

PART FOUR:

IT'S THEIR SECRET TO SHARE

Chapter Thirty-Six: Smoke

Emily never felt more alone. As she kept *The Black Susan* on the path for home everyone was quiet. The journey had been a success but the price they paid by losing their relationship with the Swimmers seemed unbearable. They sent out messages that were not answered. They stared into the ocean to see only the lonely waves. And they prayed in hopes that everything they'd just gone through had only been a bad dream. Emily spent most of her days staring at the horizon. She was eager to get everyone back to the Isle of Bryce and back to the life she remembered before this trip. It would be a much different life without Madican and Bew.

It was early morning when Emily was awake and walking the deck. She had grown accustomed to inspecting what she expected of her crew and it made her feel more confident. She saw Brett at the edge of the ship's rail peering over the side.

"Nothing exciting today is there?" Emily asked.

Brett turned to her and barely cracked a smile. Everyone on the Isle of Bryce and on Katharine's two ships had come to love Elsie and her family, and Brett was fascinated with learning about life under the surface. He and Madican had spent many hours talking about that world. Madican could paint a beautiful picture in his mind of the different colors and textures found there. If any Land Runner wanted to go live with the Swimmers it was Brett. Now his friend was gone and this new world he had been learning about was forever out of reach.

"No," he sighed.

Emily had learned so much on that trip. She learned she was in love with Madican, how to command a pirate ship, how to negotiate with an enemy, and how to tap into her inner confidence. She now needed to fine tune her leadership skills and try to bring everyone back to a happier state. Even if that was impossible for herself to do, she needed to try to encourage it with others.

"Oh," she answered. "I think we'll be home early this afternoon. Isn't that good news?"

"Yeah." He turned and looked back at the ocean. He was staring at something that caught his attention. Something small and cloudy on the horizon.

Suddenly Katharine came rushing out of her cabin. She looked as if she had seen a ghost. She was breathing heavily and looking around. She saw Emily and Brett standing together and she rushed to them yelling "The island! It's the island! It's destroyed!"

Emily squinted and looked at what Brett had been staring at. *Smoke.*

"What are you talking about?" she grabbed Katharine by both arms and shook her, making her look her in the eyes.

"The…the…island…Elsie…can't talk." Katharine stumbled over her words but Emily realized what she was saying.

Elsie must have given Katharine a message about the island. Messages travel fast with Swimmers. But Emily knew Elsie was forbidden to communicate so she must have given her just an idea of what was going on.

"Slow down and breathe," Emily said to Katharine while Brett continued to stare in the distance. The smoke was definitely coming from the direction of the isle of Bryce.

"Elsie said someone has destroyed the island. She can't tell me more because she is forbidden to talk to me. But she said to get home fast." Katharine could barely get the words out before she collapsed to her knees and began sobbing uncontrollably on the deck of the ship. The crew had stopped their duties and focused their attention on her. Emily left Katharine's side for a moment to look for a spyglass. Sensing what she was looking for, Katharine pulled one out of her breast pocket and handed it to her. "Here, look for yourself."

Emily didn't want to look. But she slowly lifted the spyglass to her eye. She still held out a slight bit of hope that maybe that smoke was not coming from the Isle of Bryce.

When the image came into view, she saw what she had dreaded.

They decided the best course would be for Emily to take *The Black Susan* to the back side of the island and Katharine would arrive with *Billlie Jean* on the main side. This way they could surprise someone if they were still there. Emily remembered the small boat she had found hidden in the vines at the edge of the beach. Those letters...JL. She couldn't figure out what it meant but she assumed it belonged to whoever destroyed her island. She wondered about Pearl and the others on the island and if they were okay.

The Black Susan made her way slowly toward the back of the island. Emily kept watch for rogue boats or anything unusual. Close to the shore she thought she saw the feet of a Swimmer crest the surface of the water as he dove deep, but she couldn't be sure. Finally, the boat was anchored down securely and the small travel boat lowered into the water. Emily took five of her crew and headed toward the shore.

The small crew rowed the little boat into the sand on the beach. They all got out and pulled it up, tying it to a young palm tree to ensure it wouldn't drift back out. Once the island was secured they would take *The Black Susan* to the front of the island and dock her on the main dock.

Emily stared up at the island. Her feet were back on the beach where she and Madican used to run. She looked for the paths that led up and over the hills and into the small village and Jesse's Place. She scanned the edge of the beach but didn't see anything out of the ordinary. Realizing the vines to the left had been the hiding place for that small boat, she ran over to see if by chance it was still there. She pushed the vines back but didn't see anything. She took a deep breath and tried to determine what she needed to inspect next. Her drawings! Of course! She ran to the other side of the small beach and found her narrow path that led up to the secret cave. The vines looked disheveled and the ground was disturbed. It looked like the area Madican had showed her where Bew was taken, only this was a different path. Emily knew someone had been there and felt sick to her stomach. *Please be there, please be there*, she thought to herself. She reached the edge of the cave and pushed back the foliage that had grown over the entrance and provided camouflage to her hiding spot. Her eyes adjusted to the lack of light as she peered into the darkness. She was scared to let herself look at the small ledge nestled into the side of the cave wall. But when she did, she saw the journal was missing. Someone had taken her drawings.

She wouldn't let herself think the journal was actually gone at first. She tried to reason with herself and questioned if she had left it in a different cave. She needed to check the other caves anyway to ensure the supplies were still there. Surely the person or persons who set the village

SMOKE

on fire wouldn't have known about those caves. Emily left her secret cave and ran back to the beach. She stared at the jungle again and saw the entrance to two different paths. One that led to the secret caves and one that led back up to Jesse's Place and the village. She chose the caves first and ran as fast as she could through the thick vines toward the caves. The crew members were following too. This was their home as well and they were just as concerned as she was.

When they reached the caves, it was all gone. Nothing had been left. The sugar, the rum, the coffee. Everything was gone. The crew was talking amongst themselves trying to determine who could have done such a thing. Emily realized she had not heard the hogs. She closed her eyes, shushed the crew and tried to listen. There was no sound. No pigs, no chickens. Not good.

"Come on," she instructed the others and they left the caves to go in search of the animals. Not far from the caves was a small shed and corral where the islanders had kept the pigs. And next to that was a large chicken coup. Both areas were empty. By now, her heart was beating fast. She wasn't sure what to think and didn't know how she was going to tell Katharine everything was gone. She was sure Katharine would want a report from that side of the island, but she also thought Pearl and the others would have filled her in.

The smell of smoke had covered the island. It was not the normal smell she was used to. On her way up the final path that led to Jesse's Place, her mind drifted to thoughts of chocolate pies, roasted chicken, and salty air. Try as she might she just couldn't get the smoke smell out of her nose. As she approached the top of the path she saw a devastation she was not prepared for. Jesse's Place had been burned. It was only a shell. No silk curtains, no chairs or tables. The bar was charred about two feet down. Glass bottles that once held beer and rum were scattered around. Some were cracked and spilled out on the ground, and some were just lying there in the ashes. The back room where she used to sleep was gone. Everything was burned to the ground. She felt sick again.

"Peeeeaaaaarrrrlllllllll!" she yelled. Deep inside she knew Pearl wouldn't answer.

Emily just stood there for a minute while the crew was making their way toward the center of the village. She looked all around trying to imagine Pearl coming back through the town. But she didn't see her.

Instead she saw Brett hurrying toward her. He looked fearful and distraught. As he came closer he put his hands out as if to corral her and keep her from going anywhere. She instantly knew he was hiding something. Something she needed to see but that he wanted to keep from her.

"Emily, I..." he started to talk to her, to try to reason with her, but she darted around him and began jogging toward the town. "Wait!" He tried to stop her but he knew it was inevitable she would find out. Emily ran through the sandy paths that laced the village. The buildings around her were all smoldering. As she ran she realized no one was around. The air was smoky and dry. She coughed and her eyes filled with tears. But as the breeze came in off the ocean it would part the smoke, if just for a moment, enough for her to see ahead. In the distance she could hear a woman weeping. Katharine? Pearl? As she got closer to the well in the center of the village she slowed her pace to a walk. Her legs started to feel numb as she began to realize what she was about to see. Inside she knew.

The well was ahead now about thirty feet. Laying in the sand around the well were many bodies. Emily feared these were islanders. And when she saw her crew and the crews from *Caesar's Ghost* and *Hector's Grip* covering them respectfully, using anything they could find, she knew this was her family. Everything had burned. There were no sheets or clothes to cover the bodies so the crew had found large palm fronds from the trees that flanked the courtyard. She looked around for Katharine but didn't see her. But she could hear her crying. Behind the circled wall of the well Katharine was kneeling over a large body. Emily approached and saw Katharine holding her hands to her mouth while she cried. The woman's hand was laying out from under the palm. Emily immediately recognized the black wrinkled fingers and fainted.

Small cracks of light startled Emily as she tried to awaken. "Child, you best get on up," Pearl cooed at her.

Thank goodness it had all been a dream. Without opening her eyes, she took a deep breath and tried to smell the beauty of her island home. No smoke! She slowly leaned up on one elbow and opened her eyes to see her Pearl sitting on the floor next to her cot smiling at her. "What are you doing on the floor, Pearl?"

Pearl just smiled back at her and reached out for her hand. Emily rubbed her eyes because Pearl's image was not very clear. Pearl spoke softly to her. "Child, you got things to do now."

SMOKE

"Wait, what?" Emily looked around at the back room of Jesse's Place. It wasn't charred. It was still intact. But what was Pearl talking about? Surely that was a dream. Pearl is sitting in front of her.

"Can you believe I get to go to Heaven?" Pearl chuckled to Emily. Emily didn't know what to do. She just sat there staring in disbelief. Pearl continued "Yep, the good Lord said I could give you a message then I needed to be on my way." Emily kept staring. She began to remember seeing Pearl's hand and hearing Katharine's cries. What was real?

"Emily, now listen up 'cause I don't got much time here, child. You got a job to do. You and Madican." Now Emily knew it wasn't real. Madican had gone. "I know Brett told you both about a plan that would keep the two of you together." *How did she know that?* "He and I had talked about it before you left the island. And the good Lord agrees with me. You gotta job to do. Go live your life with that young man."

It was too much to take in. Was this Pearl's spirit talking to her and giving her a message to go on with her life? She shook her head and when she reopened her eyes she saw a small fire in the corner of a large cave room. She was no longer in her cot at Jesse's Place. She was now in a cave. She recognized this. It was one of the storage caves. The one they used for sugar. She blinked her eyes and saw a lumpy figure lying next to the fire. As her eyes began to adjust she realized the cave was full of people sleeping. She sat up and looked around for Katharine. Was she awake this time? She stretched a bit and tried to make some sense of everything. She remembered Pearl and it made her cry. She saw Katharine sleeping close to the fire and Emily crept toward her. She laid down next to her and put her arms around her.

Ever alert, Katharine had awakened when Emily had first stirred. She pulled Emily in tight and asked, "Bad dream?"

Emily didn't know how to answer that. Since when was dreaming about Pearl bad? "Not sure," she finally answered.

"She talked to me too," Katharine said knowingly.

They both lay there together in silence for a long time. Both too anxious to sleep and too exhausted not too. "What did she say?" Emily finally asked.

"Well," Katharine started. She shifted up on one elbow and leaned over Emily ready to tell her everything. But she hesitated to tell her about Jean Lafitte. "Pearl told me my time on the island was finished and

I needed to go live with Jean in Barataria. She also said to give you *The Black Susan*, which I had already planned on doing, and that you had a plan too." Emily smiled at this thought. Maybe living with Madican was really going to happen.

Katharine's dream with Pearl was quick like Emily's was. But Pearl had told her what had happened on the island. Jean Lafitte's crew had come to destroy it. Jean knew the only way he could have Katharine for himself was to destroy her world so she would have no excuse but to come be with him. This had infuriated Katharine. But she wasn't sharing that with Emily. At least not right now. Pearl told her that the islanders had put up a good fight but in the end his crew was just too overpowering for them. Pearl had been the first one killed. This infuriated Katharine even more. Pearl had seen the anger and need for revenge in Katharine's eyes and it was not what the good Lord had wanted. He wanted to see her forgive him and move on without him. But Katharine had cut off the conversation and had awoken herself. But before she could, Pearl had told her about Brett's plan for Emily and Madican to be together. Katharine had agreed to hand over *The Black Susan* and its crew to Emily.

Emily smiled. "We're all going to be okay" she said.

Others in the room started to stir. Katharine laid back down and closed her eyes. "Emily," she said, "we have a long journey ahead of us. In a way it's like another chapter of our book is being written and we get to write it." Emily thought about her missing journal and the drawings she had kept. It was hard to overcome the things they'd experienced in the last couple of days. They lost their best friends, she lost the love of her life, and the woman who was like her mother, and their island home and all their possessions. Even in light of all that, she still held out hope that she would be with Madican again someday.

Chapter Thirty-Seven: Don't Fear the Ocean

They spent the day burying the dead. Pearl was first. She was buried under the rubble of Jesse's Place. Her soul and spirit would remain there forever watching over the island and any future inhabitants whether or not they knew it. Emily wondered if she would visit anyone else's dream, but was happy to think she was going to heaven with the good Lord. The rest were buried as close to their homes as possible. Katharine and Brett thought this would be the most restful for them.

At the end of the day, Brett had built another fire. This time it was in the center of the village. They had been able to make little symbols to represent each of the dead. A little something that represented each person. For Pearl it was a glass bottle of rum and a bit of silk cloth Emily had found in the ashes. For others it was small mementos like buttons or even twigs. Each item was thrown into the fire so the spirit of their souls could rise and find peace. At the end of the makeshift ceremony Emily stood to speak.

"As you know, we've all been through a horrific event. We have lost all our loved ones. Those on land have perished trying to defend our home, and those in the sea have willingly left our company for the safety of anonymity. There is no option for us who remain other than to take the two ships and set out for other lands and lives. Katharine and Brett will take a crew north toward the new Americas. They have been offered homes with Jean Lafitte on his many islands. They plan to continue the way of the pirate. Those crew members who accompany her will be given homes as well."

She paused to see the response of the small crowd. Most were looking down, grieving over their losses. She continued, "I plan to take *The Black Susan* and continue the way of the pirates as well, but we have no promise of a home life. We will have to find our own way. I will sail up the coast of Florida to Key Vacas. There are safe places for pirates there. They are welcome in their town unlike most places. I feel we can make a good home for ourselves there when we are not out on the water. Those who travel with me will be given a fair wage and a fair way of life. I will follow in Katharine's example."

Emily continued, "Tonight the souls of our island family have been sent to Peace in the heavens as our fire burns. But let us not forget the souls of our family in the sea. They still swim. Their souls are not at rest right now because they grieve with us." Now boos and moans from the crowd. Emily continued trying to display a calming nature. "As we separate our ships and our lives, we will make a promise to the Swimmers that they can always find comfort, solace, and trust amongst any of us. You all made that promise to Katharine when she brought you to live here, and now we ask you to continue that promise as you venture out." There was a slight shift in the response from the crowd now.

"The Swimmers will need to be able to know us by a familiar mark." She turned toward the fire and using a heavy cloth, lifted a branding iron out of the hot coals. The end was the letter B scrolled in old English. "This iron was used on our island to mark our possessions. It marked items we placed value on. If you have this mark on your upper arm, the Swimmers will know you are worthy of their trust because you place a value on them."

Emily handed the iron to Katharine who held it tight while Emily raised her own sleeve. She turned toward Katharine and let her mark her arm. She screamed a bit when it burnt her flesh, but she was strong enough to handle it. Katharine proceeded to mark Brett and a few others brave enough to step forward. By the end of the night everyone had been marked. Everyone had agreed to keep the secret of the Swimmers and to support them if they needed it.

Katharine was the last to be marked. After her branding, she spoke. "We have all made a delicate promise tonight, family. As we go out into the world and separate ourselves from each other, we must remember the secret will end with us. Once we are spirits in the sky, no one else can know the secret we carry. No lovers or children or friends can ever know, until the Swimmers are ready. It is their secret to share."

The night was somber as everyone knew the next day carried such weight. There was no rum to drink or food to eat except for what was on the ships. And the ships' supplies were low. Katharine would give Emily half of their supplies because she knew she would have plenty on her way to Jean's. But since Emily had further to go, it was better for her to have more supplies. The Spanish had been seen a lot around the area of Florida so Katharine assumed Emily would have plenty to plunder on her journey to Key Vacas.

"Emily!" Katharine called for her across the dock. Emily turned and saw Katharine coming toward her. This goodbye was something Emily had dreaded. The ships had been readied and Emily was about to set sail.

"My, you've really come a long way, young lady," Katharine complimented her. Emily blushed and shook off the compliment quickly. She didn't want all the fuss going to her head.

"I don't know." Emily corrected her. "I guess I've had a great role model" She couldn't stand it anymore and threw her arms around Katharine's neck. "Oh, Katharine! I'm going to miss you sooooo much!"

"Emily, I'm going to miss you too, hon." Katharine was being sweet, which Emily was not used to. "But I would never want to stand in the way of your future."

"Yours either," Emily cried, realizing this sounded silly.

Katharine pulled back and held Emily by both arms and looked straight in her eyes "Don't fear the ocean or anything in it. *The Black Susan* was meant for you. She is fast and strong and will protect you well. I know there will always be a Swimmer nearby if you need one. All you need to do is ask and they will be there. Forbidden or not, they still love us too. Live your life, Emily and be strong. But most importantly...." Katharine lowered her hands from Emily's arms and held her hands tight and close to her chest, "Be happy."

And that was that. Katharine dropped Emily's hands and walked away. Her ship would be leaving soon too and she needed to prepare. Emily watched as Katharine walked back up the dock to the shore and up the path toward the village.

Emily sailed *The Black Susan* toward the east. As she was leaving she watched the island in the distance grow smaller and smaller. The smoke had long since cleared away and all that was left now were the ghosts who would stay to watch over the island and play with the other spirits in the sky. Emily turned and walked to the front of the ship. From this moment on, she decided, she would always look ahead and never behind. She was determined to find a new place where she could live, love and walk along the tidelines.

TIDELINES

Epilogue

She rubbed the chalk residue between her fingers while she watched the men in the room. Long ago her captain taught her how to conceal her identity and dress like a man. She hovered in the back corner, slowing sketching in her journal while watching the air grow thick with the smells of the storm coming. Everyone's excitement was stifled. No one shared their expectations or allowed the others in the room to see their anxiety. They all knew it was coming. They all watched the door, anxiously awaiting the news. Some smoked their pipes and others drank their rum. But the competition was deadly, so they all sat in quiet anticipation. Storms meant ships would sink. Sunken ships meant treasure. And treasure hunters were plentiful in these parts. Wreckers, they called themselves. Salvaging what they could of the merchandise. It was dangerous, it fed a man's greed. Dying sailors were often passed over in an effort to save the trunk full of gold that was sinking fast. But on the other side of the tavern, in the midst of it all, he was there. He was there with his Swimmer friends, taking advantage of the needs of the Land Runners. He was a part of this dreary picture she was capturing on paper.

She heard the wind pick up and it shook the small building they were all huddled in. Suddenly the men stiffened and sat up a little straighter in their chairs. Someone was running towards the building and they had all heard it. The small door was made of five planks strung together with old rope. It barely held together when the young boy flung it open and yelled to everyone: "Wreck Ashore!!"

Made in the USA
Las Vegas, NV
07 November 2022